Also by Eve Wersocki Morris

The Bird Singers

THE WILDSTORM CURSE

EVE WERSOCKI MORRIS

Hodder
Children's
Books

HODDER CHILDREN'S BOOKS

First published in Great Britain in 2023 by Hodder & Stoughton

1 3 5 7 9 10 8 6 4 2

A CIP catalogue record for this book
is available from the British Library.

ISBN 978 1 444 96334 2

Typeset in Egyptian 505 BT by Avon DataSet Ltd, Alcester, Warwickshire

Printed and bound in Great Britain by Clays Ltd, Elcograf S.p.A.

The paper and board used in this book
are made from wood from responsible sources.

MIX
Paper from
responsible sources
FSC® C104740

Hodder Children's Books
An imprint of Hachette Children's Group
Part of Hodder & Stoughton Limited
Carmelite House
50 Victoria Embankment
London EC4Y 0DZ

An Hachette UK Company
www.hachette.co.uk

www.hachettechildrens.co.uk

For Mum, thank you for reading my stories and checking my spelling

For everyone who made those summers at B possible – 'People full of heart, each playing out their part'

Not all stories bring good to our world.
Some tales will fester, like weeds in a wood
Like thorns, bring darkness and block out the light
Beware the shadow that clouds your mind
– And beware the one who conjures it.

CHAPTER ONE

Kallie Tamm was never meant to arrive at Wildstorm Theatre Camp in the dead of night. However, after two missed trains, a broken-down bus and five stale sandwiches, it was dark when Kallie and her mum finally reached Littlewick-on-Marsh station. All Kallie knew was that they were somewhere in the Gloucestershire countryside and she was further from home than she had ever been before.

The darkness outside the taxi windows was thick as smoke. Kallie peered out, nervousness bubbling in her stomach, searching for some clue to the place she would be spending her summer holiday. The night gave nothing away. The occasional flicker of light from a cottage window was all that disturbed the blackness.

Kallie's mum sat beside her, leaning forward every ten minutes to remind the taxi driver of the address: Hollowstar House in the village of Merricombe. Kallie had never even heard of Merricombe before a month ago. She liked the name, though – saying it felt like chanting a spell.

At thirteen years old, teachers sometimes mistook Kallie as shy. She could often be quiet but that was only because her head was buzzing with stories and speeches for plays. Kallie's mum said she had a gift for daydreaming. But it was a gift that sometimes made it hard to make friends. And Kallie would know no one at the theatre camp. The thought made her insides plummet.

'We're here,' the taxi driver grunted.

Kallie looked out of the window. She could see the outline of a tall house, so wrapped up in plant life it could have been part of the hedge. There was a brass star above the front door. Kallie's mum prodded her out of the taxi.

'I think this is the place,' muttered her mum, looking up at the shadowy windows. There was no one around.

Kallie glanced up and down the lane. There were no street lights. No moon. The road ahead vanished into pitch black. It was as if the house was the only thing in existence and if Kallie took two steps forward, she'd fall off the earth into nothingness.

'Look – what's that?' Kallie stepped a little closer to her mum.

A light had appeared, like a single glowing eye. It moved swiftly closer, growing larger, until Kallie realised it was a torch.

'Kallie Tamm? I thought it might be you,' came a voice.

'We're here for the theatre camp,' Kallie's mum called back.

A figure stepped into the taxi's headlamps. Kallie recognised her from the website: Jackie Masters, the director of Wildstorm Theatre Camp. Black-haired and uncommonly tall. She looked forbidding.

'You're late,' Jackie observed, her mouth a thin line of disapproval.

Kallie was always very interested in people's voices. Jackie had a hard voice, like a hammer knocking on nails.

'We're so sorry. We missed the change at Reading,' Kallie's mum stammered. 'I've got to get the last train back to London. Early shift tomorrow.' She turned to Kallie. 'You'll be OK, won't you?'

'Yes.' Kallie nodded, but her heart was racing painfully. 'I'll – it'll be fine, Mum. Don't worry.'

Her mum squeezed her shoulders.

'Have the best time, babe,' her mum whispered, giving Kallie a final hug. 'I'm so proud of you. Love you.'

Then she was gone, the taxi headlamps sweeping away into the blackness. Kallie stared after it, panic rising inside her. Everything was happening so quickly.

'You're too late to meet the rest of the cast tonight,' said Jackie, scooping up Kallie's bag as if it weighed nothing. 'You've had a long journey. You need a good night's sleep.'

Kallie felt light-headed and empty, as if half her body had been whisked away with her mum. Maybe this hadn't been a good idea after all. Dazedly, she followed Jackie into Hollowstar House.

The house was a muddle of wooden beams, sloping ceilings and cushioned cubbyholes. Kallie almost forgot her nervousness as she stepped over the threshold. There were paintings and old maps lining the walls and mountainous bookshelves full of playscripts.

Despite her great height, Jackie moved quickly through the rooms and low doorways. Kallie hurried to catch up, breathing in the dusty warmth. She was just starting to get excited when Jackie spoke.

'The house is off limits to the cast,' she said briskly. 'You'll eat your meals out here.'

Her heart sinking, Kallie followed Jackie into the dark garden. A trail of fairy lights marked a path heading away from the house. Kallie would have found it beautiful had it not been for the darkness and the silence, still pressing in all around them. Jackie set off between the lights.

'The Wildstormers camp in the meadow,' said Jackie, with a jerk of her torch.

'I don't have a tent,' said Kallie, half hoping Jackie would send her back to Hollowstar House.

'That won't be necessary.'

Kallie never considered that the theatre camp would involve actual camping. She'd never slept in a tent before.

At the end of the garden there was a hut with an orange lamp outside. This was the bathroom and shower – thankfully it had an electric light – and Jackie waited outside while Kallie hurriedly brushed her teeth. The night felt even darker when she emerged.

'Everyone must be inside their tents at ten,' said Jackie, gesturing to the meadow beyond the hut. 'I advise getting your rest: putting on a play is hard work.'

Kallie could make out the spectral outlines of several tents. There were torches moving inside them, darting like fireflies, and the low rumble of voices. Kallie's throat tightened. She was glad she wasn't meeting the other kids tonight. The beam of Jackie's torch picked out a tent at the far end of the meadow.

'You can take that one. It's small but you'll fit. Here.'

The director placed her torch in Kallie's hand. She paused, then gave her a surprisingly kind smile.

'You'll get used to our ways soon enough.' Jackie gave her a curt nod. 'Welcome to Wildstorm Theatre Camp, Kallie. Sleep well.'

And Jackie strode away, leaving Kallie alone in the dark.

Chapter Two

Two eyes opened, bright as fire.

Something was stirring in the ancient woodland above Merricombe. Less than one mile from where Kallie Tamm slept an uneasy sleep in the meadow behind Hollowstar House.

Deep within the undergrowth – deeper than even the rabbits and voles dared to go – in a thicket of ferns and grizzled roots, two bright eyes blinked. Nothing else moved.

Then the eyes flickered from side to side. They could see again. After all this time. Sleep, which had clung like a cloak for so long, was falling away. As the eyes moved back and forth, they saw the shapes of trees and patches of night sky.

It knew this woodland, these trees, this moonless sky. But everything was foggy. How it had come to be – and what it had been – was still a mystery. It was thirsty. Hungry. The instinct to hunt was rising inside it.

The eyes blinked again, trying to make sense of everything. But it was so thin and weak it could barely think. It was little more than a shadow, crouching in a mossy nook. Even so, the woodland feared it. Leaves shuddered and wild flowers shrank and cowered.

The shadow's memory was swirling like a whirlpool. It saw a flash of light, the sweaty-faced villagers and then . . . terrible, blinding pain. Anger flared within the shadow and the eyes blazed in the gloom.

It remembered now. It knew why it had awoken – why it had returned.

CHAPTER THREE

Kallie dreamt she was in a forest at dusk. The trees around her were grey and the grass was like smoke. A chill prickled her skin as she walked amongst the strange landscape. And then she heard something: footsteps coming slowly closer and closer. She started to run but it felt like she was wading through sludge – she couldn't run fast enough and the footsteps were growing louder behind her. At last, she reached a clearing and ahead she saw a tree stump, illuminated in the starlight. She moved closer. On the stump lay a green feathered quill. There were shouts behind her, threats on the cold air. As Kallie reached out a hand for the quill, something seized her from behind and she was dragged backwards into blackness . . .

When Kallie awoke, hours later, the dream faded from her mind like summer mist. Sunlight was shining through the walls of the tent. She rubbed her eyes. Outside she could hear the coo of a wood pigeon and a distant bleating of sheep. It was as if the tent had been transported to a new location in the night.

It was cosy and homely inside the tent. Kallie hadn't noticed it last night; she'd been too busy stumbling around in the dark trying to pull her pyjama leggings on to her arms.

The tent wasn't one of those plastic ones she'd seen on TV, which deflated whenever there was a gust of wind. It was made of thick white canvas, held up by a wooden frame. The sleeping bag lay snugly on a foam mattress, which was covered in a beaded blanket. There were colourful lights strung over the ceiling connected to a battery pack switch, which made them glitter like jewels. At the foot of her mattress was a box with *Wildstorm Theatre Camp* printed across the top; inside she found snack bars, a notebook, a tin water bottle and a tiny torch. Camping really wasn't as bad as she'd thought! Kallie felt excitement stir inside her.

The camp had been her idea. Kallie wanted to be a playwright, ever since she'd visited Shakespeare's Globe on a school trip two years ago, and fallen in love with theatre. It was like nothing else. In the theatre, she'd seen people fly on invisible cords, vanish into thin air and change their appearance with a click of their fingers. The playwright's words were turned into real-life adventures right in front of the audience's eyes.

Since that school trip, Kallie had been writing her own plays, about fairy tales and monsters mostly. She'd perform them for her mum, with the help of their two cats, Puck and Mustard-Seed. The cats might not be any good at learning lines but they always looked great in their costumes (which Kallie made from old clothes and newspaper).

But she longed to be part of a real play – preferably one where the set wasn't made of sofa cushions and a laundry basket. Kallie's school didn't do a school play and their drama class was taught by the sports coach; the only acting they did in Mr Ward's classes was when he got them to re-enact the football team's latest goals.

So Kallie had started researching drama clubs and theatre camps for the summer holidays. Her mum would be out at her cleaning shifts and Kallie would be alone in the flat. The only problem was everything she found was too expensive and everywhere required an audition. Kallie wasn't a bad actor – she liked coming up with characters and was pretty good at doing different voices – but reading something aloud for the first time was tricky: familiar words would look nonsensical, and sentences kept rearranging themselves. Last time she'd read aloud in English, she had messed up easy words, skipped sentences by mistake and mispronounced the main character's name. She still went hot with embarrassment every time she remembered the giggling from the back of the classroom.

Kallie had almost given up hope when she spotted a flyer in the school library:

WILDSTORM THEATRE CAMP

Are you 12-14 years old?
Do you love theatre?

Join the cast and rehearse a play to be performed on the last weekend of July in the historic Merricombe Theatre in Gloucestershire

No audition needed

And the best part . . .

Playwriting Competition

The winner of the best 10-page script will win a free place at Wildstorm this summer

Kallie didn't pause to wonder what a flyer for a Gloucestershire theatre camp was doing in a London school. She immediately checked out the Wildstorm Theatre Camp website and saw there was still time to apply. Kallie knew this was her chance. She spent the next week working on her new play, writing and rewriting pages at breaktime and reading and rereading it every night before she went to sleep. After her mum had checked it for spelling and Kallie had typed it up on the school library computer, *The Unlikely Hero* was ready to send off. Kallie had thrown everything she loved into it – adventure and peril; bravery and friendship; a terrifying villain who came to a sticky end! She liked it but she had no idea if it was good enough to win. So when Jackie Masters emailed telling Kallie she was the winner, she thought she might explode with happiness. That had only been two weeks ago. The memory of her mum dancing around the flat in celebration still made her swell with pride.

Kallie unzipped her sleeping bag. It didn't sound like anyone else was up yet and if she was lucky she'd have a chance to explore alone. Kallie dressed quickly in her usual black jeans and favourite black-and-white top. She hastily combed her hair with her fingers. She had very long brown hair, which was always getting knotted. She wriggled into her trainers and stepped outside.

The sun was dawning bright and rosy. It must still be very early, she thought.

The meadow was a lot smaller than it had looked in the dark. There were ten canvas tents; most of them were much larger than Kallie's tent – the bell-shaped one in the opposite corner could probably sleep about five or six. There was another tent with *STAFF* painted on the side. Colourful bunting was strung out between them, fluttering in the morning breeze. Thick hedges hugged the sides of the meadow, daisies scattered at their roots, and beyond Kallie could see fields slanting away towards a wood. The air was fresh and she couldn't help smiling.

She opened the gate to the garden and saw Hollowstar House properly for the first time. It was older than anything she'd ever seen. Ivy spread so densely across its walls, burrowing into every crack, that Kallie thought if you took the house away the ivy would hold its shape perfectly.

She walked quietly towards the house; the fairy lights that had marked their way last night were woven into purple hydrangeas lining the path. On the lawn in front of the house were two wooden tables covered with a gigantic patchwork canopy, protecting them from the morning dew. There was no one around.

Kallie squinted up at the roof. There were dark markings under the eaves and around the windows. Curious symbols like flowers, six thin petals fanning out in a perfect circle. Kallie felt a thrill of curiosity.

She took a step closer, then all of a sudden a dark shape sprang on to the path ahead of her. She stumbled backwards, half-scared, before she realised it was a small black cat. The cat stared at her with stern green eyes. There was something about its calculating expression that reminded Kallie of the Wildstorm director, Jackie.

'I'm just having a look around,' said Kallie, as the cat continued to stare.

The cat turned and trotted away, but when it reached the side of Hollowstar House it looked back at her before flicking around the corner. Her interest piqued, Kallie hurried after it. There was a narrow path between the house wall and the hedge – but instead of going straight and coming out on the road, the cat veered to the left and disappeared into a gap in the hedge.

Kallie followed and found herself in a thicket of trees. There was a building a short distance away, just visible between the trunks. The cat bounded ahead and Kallie hurried to keep up. The trees loomed above her; their branches clawed up towards the sunny sky. There was something strange and enchanting about these trees and she felt a peculiar chill creep over her. She wasn't scared exactly but they set her imagination spinning. The wood felt full of stories and secrets waiting to be uncovered.

The cat had stopped, watching her.

Kallie placed a hand on a trunk. These trees reminded her of something . . . the dream! She'd almost forgotten about it. The grey woodland and the green quill on the tree stump. And there had been someone chasing her—

There was a noise – footsteps were approaching behind her – and Kallie whirled around.

'Don't touch him! He'll take your eyes out and eat them for breakfast!'

A girl, who looked about thirteen, was jogging up the path from the house.

'I'm sorry,' Kallie stammered. 'I got up early and didn't know where to go and—'

'Oh, you're a new Stormer! Ah, no trouble then!' The girl's face broke into a wide, open smile. She bent down and scooped up the cat. 'Thought you were from the village – snooping. Some of them don't like it, do they? Think it's bad luck and all that rubbish! The Historical Society are the worst of the snoops. But we'll show them, won't we?'

Kallie blinked at her. This girl was smaller than Kallie, with short curly blonde hair. She spoke like a whirlwind but in a way that made Kallie feel instantly like she was part of the plan – even though she had no idea what this plan might be.

'Sorry but – who are you?' said Kallie.

'I'm jumping five steps ahead. I'm sorry! I'm Emilia. The cat's Smudge.'

'I'm Kallie,' she said, reaching out to scratch Smudge under the chin. The cat purred in greeting.

'Poor Smudge,' observed Emilia, 'I say he's fierce to give him a good reputation, you know, but he's actually just a fluff-brained sweetie. Couldn't frighten a mouse. But he likes to think he guards this place.'

She nodded to the building through the trees. They moved closer and Kallie's heart started to drum with excitement. It was made of a weather-worn grey stone with diamond-patterned windows beneath a slate roof. There was a grandeur about the place. It felt just as alive as the woodland around it.

'Is this the Merricombe Theatre?' said Kallie in an awed tone that made Emilia grin. 'What did you say was bad luck?' she asked curiously.

Emilia blew a curl out of her face and sighed.

'It's the theatre, you see,' said Emilia. 'The villagers think it's cursed – because of the witch.'

CHAPTER FOUR

Breakfast was served out of the kitchen door at Hollowstar House. There were trays of sizzling eggs, sausages and bacon, homemade hash browns, mushrooms and tomatoes, vegetarian sausages (which looked much better than anything Kallie had at home) and a small cauldron of baked beans. All cooked by a crotchety old man in a flat cap, who Emilia referred to as Burn.

Kallie and Emilia took their steaming plates out into the garden. Smudge stayed behind to beg for scraps. The sun had settled in a blue sky and the air was sweet with wild flowers. Emilia pointed to the end of a table and they sat down opposite each other.

'The best seats in the garden,' said Emilia, tapping her nose. 'The table is less wonky at this end.'

It was still early but a slow stream of Wildstormers were beginning to wander up from the campsite, most of them wearing pyjamas under their hoodies.

'So why do the villagers think the theatre is cursed?' Kallie asked, tucking into her breakfast. 'And what did you say about a witch?'

Emilia grinned. 'I knew you'd be interested in that,' she said. 'You're a writer and writers are always curious.'

'Yeah, I want to be a playwright – but how did you know?'

Emilia's eyes sparkled. 'You've got that look – the daydreaming, misty-eyed writer look.'

'Really?' said Kallie, amused. 'It's probably just hunger. Mum calls it my "food face".'

Emilia snorted into her mushrooms. 'That is hilarious! I love it!' She chortled. 'And actually, I saw your application. That's how I know.'

'How did you see my application?'

'My mum runs Wildstorm.' Emilia shrugged. 'I thought you knew.'

'Your mum is Jackie?' asked Kallie, unable to hide her surprise.

Jackie's forbidding stare was worlds away from Emilia's bubbly friendliness. Kallie wondered if they got on.

'It's OK to find her a bit scary,' said Emilia, 'everyone does. She'd kill me if she knew I'd been looking at the applications! Your play was amazing, by the way. *The Unlikely Hero.*'

'You read my play?' Kallie felt suddenly hot. 'Has everyone read it?'

'Oh no. Just me being a snoop – it's so good! Really! I loved it.'

'Thanks. Um . . . So what else do you know about the witch?' pressed Kallie, feeling uncomfortable in the spotlight.

Emilia took a gulp of orange squash and cleared her throat dramatically.

'Her name was Ellsabet Graveheart. And she lived in Merricombe four hundred years ago when the theatre was first built. The story goes that Ellsabet cursed the theatre with evil magic!'

'And the villagers think it might still be cursed?'

'Oh yeah!' Emilia rolled her eyes. 'The villagers are always going on about Ellsabet and the curse. She's like a local celebrity – they sell Ellsabet the Witch tea towels and Ellsabet the Witch socks.'

'What do they think about Wildstorm using the theatre?'

'This is the first year we're actually in the theatre,' said Emilia, her eyes shining. 'It wasn't ready last year – had to have a ton of building work done – so we did the show in this huge tent in the field, which was awesome. But the Historical Society aren't happy about Mum opening up the theatre – bunch of old toads! They sent Mum this long list of things we're not allowed to do. Mr Mildew, he's the head of the Historical Society, loves making up stupid rules. He tried to get Mum to sign something to say we wouldn't talk above a whisper in the theatre!'

'What happened?' asked Kallie.

'Mum flushed his letter down the loo and told him she wasn't having any of it.' Emilia grinned. 'Mum won't let the Historical Society boss her around. Great-Aunt Meryl left her the theatre and Hollowstar House two years ago – she owns it. They can't make her do anything.'

'And . . .' Kallie swallowed. 'Do *you* think the theatre is cursed?'

'Nah. No way. It's just a story. A story the villagers have been milking for four hundred years.'

Emilia pulled a face and Kallie laughed. The idea of a legendary witch in Merricombe made Kallie's heart sing – she was already itching to write it down in her notebook.

'But what did Ellsabet Graveheart do?' asked Kallie excitedly.

'Witchy stuff, I guess,' said Emilia, 'spells and potions and things. To be honest, I don't really know. Mum doesn't like talking about Ellsabet the Witch – she says the villagers are fools to believe it. She—'

But they were interrupted by a mocking voice behind them. 'I can't believe Emilia Masters doesn't know the story of Ellsabet Graveheart!'

Kallie looked up to see a boy standing above them – he looked about a year older than her, with glossy black hair and high cheekbones.

'I thought your family were supposed to be local,' he said disdainfully. 'Even I know the story.'

'Oh, good for you, Marlow!' Emilia shot back sarcastically.

'And who is your new friend here?' Marlow's eyes roamed to Kallie.

'This is Kallie. She's the winner of the Wildstorm Playwriting Prize,' said Emilia proudly.

'*The Unlikely Hero*?' sneered Marlow. 'I heard Violet talking about it. I'd have called it the very unlikely hero, if you ask me.' He looked Kallie up and down. 'Who wears black in summer?'

He cracked a wicked smile.

'Someone who doesn't care what nosy people like you think,' said Kallie coolly, before she could stop herself.

Emilia snorted behind her hand and Marlow flushed.

'Think you're such a smartie, huh?' he sneered. 'People said Ellsabet Graveheart was a smartie too and you know what happened to her . . . ? Oh wait. You *don't* know!'

He laughed.

'Oh, grow up!' Emilia sighed. 'We'd like to finish our breakfast in peace, if you don't mind.'

The boy gave Kallie another withering look before flouncing away.

'Marlow Lee,' explained Emilia. 'Best ignore him. He's just bitter that you won the prize. So pathetic. Marlow walks around like he's the star of his own one-man show.'

'But he seems so sweet and shy,' said Kallie sarcastically.

Emilia guffawed with laughter and Kallie grinned. But even as she smiled, Kallie's heart was plummeting. She watched Marlow join a large group by the kitchen door. From the way he dressed, she was fairly certain that Marlow Lee hadn't needed to win the free place at Wildstorm. More Wildstormers were walking up from the campsite now; most of them waved good morning to Marlow's group as they passed. Kallie fiddled with her T-shirt. She hadn't thought about the fact that everyone would already know each other. She was quickly regretting her come-back to Marlow; she didn't want to make an enemy on her first day.

'How long has Wildstorm been going on?' Kallie asked, watching Emilia polishing off her bacon in two bites.

'This is the second year,' said Emilia. 'You should have come last year. We did this play set under the sea and everyone was dressed in blue bubble-wrap! It was amazing!'

'And has everyone come back again?'

'Not everyone,' muttered Emilia, and for the first time she looked sad.

Kallie wanted to ask more but she didn't want to pry.

'Do you think Marlow really does know the story of the witch?' she asked.

Emilia huffed. 'He's probably just being annoying – as usual. But if you really want to know more, I'm sure we can find out. It's like the most important story in Merricombe history. Just don't let my mum hear you talking about it or she'll go off on one of her rants.'

'Does your dad help at Wildstorm too?'

'Nope. Don't know my dad,' said Emilia, unconcerned, now attacking her baked beans.

'Me neither,' said Kallie and Emilia looked up.

They shared a brief smile. Kallie didn't often think about her dad. He'd left before she was born and there wasn't much to say about him. Instead, Kallie entertained Emilia with funny stories from home, including the time Puck had eaten Kallie's birthday cake and Mustard-Seed had fallen in the toilet. Emilia listened and laughed as if she knew them already.

'Home is me, Mum and Violet – Mum's partner,' shared Emilia. 'And Smudge too, of course. We're a house of drama nerds!'

Kallie grinned. It was impossible not to like Emilia. She had a voice like a babbling brook. Her way of talking made Kallie feel like they'd been friends for years – and hadn't just met two hours ago.

A clanging noise made Kallie jump. A woman wearing a purple jumpsuit had come out of the house, banging on a small drum.

'Everyone meet in the meadow in fifteen minutes,' she called. 'Brush your teeth. Get dressed! Don't be late!'

Emilia grinned, her eyes sparkling again. Kallie managed a smile back but inside she was growing numb with nerves.

As they took their plates back to the kitchen, Burn

was accepting a delivery of fifty boxes of biscuits from a man in an orange apron.

'You kids excited to get started?' The man smiled. 'The play you did last year tickled me pink, I'll be honest with you.'

'Thanks, Mr Dixson.' Emilia grinned back. 'He's from the Marmalade Café,' she added as an aside to Kallie. 'Best biscuits and cakes in Merricombe.'

Kallie nodded but her mind was already down in the meadow. This was it – her first day at Wildstorm Theatre Camp was about to begin.

'Hey, Em!' The woman in the jumpsuit hailed them. 'Carry these to the meadow, will you?'

She gestured to a pair of crates on the doorstep full of objects, including a crown, a stuffed crow, a neck ruff and a fluffy feather boa. Kallie stepped forward to help but then she spotted something that made her freeze. Dread flooded her. Poking out of one of the crates was a green feathered quill. Exactly the same quill that Kallie had seen in her dream.

Chapter Five

The shadow in the wood had grown stronger. It had ventured further out and now lingered amongst the sweet chestnut trees, keeping close to the knotted trunks. The eyes blinked, camouflaged amongst the spots of light on the mossy bark.

It needed something to feed on. Something to revive it. It felt good to hunt after all this time.

Its memories were still messy. The shadow, lurking at the foot of the chestnut trees, had not yet pieced together the jigsaw of events that had led to this moment. It knew why it had returned. To punish those who had wronged it. The sweetest of all quests. But the details were still distant. It would need help to fill the memory gaps.

The shadow was still too weak to travel far. The woodland and the surrounding meadows still smelt the same but below in the village there were new sounds and smells that the shadow did not recognise.

A crunch of footsteps broke through the hush. There were three figures walking up ahead. Three boys. Two were wielding sticks and jabbing at low-hanging branches. The third moved with hunched shoulders, talking quietly.

'. . . don't want me to go to the theatre camp.' The boy's words travelled on the wind. 'I don't know what I can do.'

The theatre? Now this was interesting.

Was it possible the theatre was still standing? After all this time? The eyes glinted as the boys came closer and closer.

'Dunno what the fuss is all about,' said another boy. 'But if you really want to do it – chat to your dad again.'

'He won't listen. I just feel bad, you know.'

They were so engaged in their conversation that they did not spare a glance for the chestnut trees. Now was the shadow's chance. It could feel the hunger growing inside – it was ready for more mischief.

The three boys didn't notice the shadow approach.

Until it was too late.

CHAPTER SIX

Jackie Masters stood in the centre of the campsite, facing the Wildstormers; she had a knack of looking everyone in the eye at once.

The morning had turned hotter. The distant woodland was hazy with sunlight and murmuring insects. Kallie had never seen countryside like this before. When they did go on holiday, Kallie and her mum usually went to the beach for the day. The magnificent greenery of Gloucestershire felt like stepping inside a fairy tale.

The Wildstorm cast was made up of twenty boys and girls, all twelve to fourteen years old. Kallie had been half-expecting a crowd of Marlow Lee lookalikes, all jostling for attention, but everyone seemed relaxed and friendly – most of them waved to Emilia as they took their place in the circle – and there was excitement on every face.

Kallie hadn't said anything about the quill to Emilia. Announcing that you'd just seen an object from a dream was weird to say the least. Dreams didn't come true. Maybe it was a coincidence? Maybe all Emilia's talk about Ellsabet the Witch and ancient curses had made Kallie's imagination spin out of control.

'Can I have everyone's attention?'

Kallie tried to focus on what the theatre camp director was saying.

'Welcome to our second year at Wildstorm.' Jackie flashed a hawkish smile at them. 'Those who came last year will know that we are here for one reason only: to create a superb production on Saturday night. And this year we will be performing in the newly renovated theatre.' A flutter of anticipation passed through the circle. 'We have five days.' She held up a calendar with *5 DAYS TO GO* written on the first sheet. 'If anyone needs a reminder, I will be putting this on the kitchen door.' She paused. 'This is not school. I am not here to be your teacher; I am here to be your director. And I expect a high level of professionalism from you, the actors.'

Marlow Lee stood a little taller as if hoping to get a gold star for his 'professionalism', but Kallie was willing to bet that Jackie wasn't the type to have favourites.

'New Stormers, be warned: we have three rules,' said Jackie, her voice stern. 'First rule: every role is equally important and I want everyone giving their best. Second rule: do not leave the grounds of Hollowstar House without permission. Third rule: never go into the theatre alone. If anyone does not follow these rules, they will be in serious trouble.'

Her words hung in the air.

'I'll be announcing this year's play after lunch,' concluded Jackie, and there was a disappointed mumble from the crowd. 'But now let's meet the team who will be helping you.'

Jackie gestured to the colourful crew of adults at the side of the meadow. There was the purple-jumpsuited Violet, the assistant director; Ray, the set designer; Dotty, the costumer; and a few other cheerful helpers.

'Do you know anything about this year's play?' Kallie leant towards Emilia.

'No way, Mum's been keeping it top secret,' Emilia whispered back. 'I haven't even got a sniff of it this year.'

Violet clapped her hands. She had a bright, songlike voice and twinkling eyes.

'Everyone ready for some warm-up games?' Violet beamed.

Kallie lost Emilia in the crowd as everyone started walking around in a wide circle. There was one other new Wildstormer: a boy called Ivan, who had a slightly lopsided haircut. The two of them exchanged awkward smiles whenever they passed – the only two outsiders in a sea of friends. Kallie tried not to be too self-conscious as they played name games, silly games comparing shoe sizes and learnt a funny song. Unlike at school, there was no embarrassment or eye-rolling, everyone just got stuck in and, after a few rounds, Kallie was actually enjoying herself. After an hour, everyone flopped on to the grass, breathless and laughing.

'Now that we're all warmed up,' said Jackie, 'I want you all to choose an object.' She gestured to the crates of props – Kallie could see the green quill fluttering in the breeze and her heart leapt. 'You will have fifteen minutes,' Jackie explained, 'to come up with an opening speech inspired by that object before sharing it with the rest of the group. Theatre is all about storytelling. I want you to take us on a journey and leave us wanting to hear more. Time starts . . . now.'

There was a surge towards the crates. Kallie saw Marlow snatch the crown from under someone's nose and march away. Kallie headed for the green quill, filled with curiosity.

'Are you sure you want that?'

Jackie was standing behind her.

'Yes!' said Kallie, so quickly she was worried she had sounded rude.

Jackie raised an eyebrow.

'I – I like pens,' stammered Kallie, feeling stupid. 'And a quill is basically an old pen.'

Jackie raised the other eyebrow.

'Your play for the competition was exceptionally accomplished,' said Jackie. 'I'm expecting good things, Kallie.'

Kallie garbled a 'thank you', but Jackie had already swept away. Emilia's mum was clearly passionate about theatre, but she was nonetheless rather stern.

Everyone had spread out over the meadow. Emilia had picked the stuffed crow and was stroking it thoughtfully. Kallie leant against her own tent with her new Wildstorm notebook. She twirled the quill in her fingers; it was soft as velvet. The quill didn't *feel* strange. Perhaps she'd seen it in Hollowstar House the night before without realising it and that's what had sparked the dream. The thought calmed her.

She already knew exactly what story she could tell about this quill – the idea was emerging like a map from the darkness. She started scribbling away, not bothering to keep her handwriting neat or worry about her spelling.

When time was up, Kallie watched, in awe, as her fellow cast members performed their opening speeches to the group. They were all very good. A tall, blonde boy did a speech from the perspective of a garden gnome and a girl with ginger curls gave a tale about a dancing teacup. Then Marlow swaggered forward, the crown on his head, and told a story of a prince plotting to kill his father and take over the kingdom. His performance got a couple of whoops from the crowd.

'Show-off!' Emilia mouthed at Kallie.

'Kallie, why don't you come up?' said Jackie.

Kallie stood, trying not to look too nervous. She looked down at her speech, focusing on her story.

'This quill belongs to a storyteller,' Kallie said and as soon as she'd started, the upturned faces vanished as she stepped into her imagination. 'Her story is one of hope and fear. She is on the run – all she has is her quill and a sack of parchment. The storyteller has escaped in the dead of night from the Northern Kingdom, ruled by a cruel tyrant, and she is seeking safety with the benevolent Southern Lord. Because this storyteller has a secret. Her stories have a stupendous power. Her words can warm the coldest soul. Her stories calm the fearful and fill people with bravery in moments of terror. But the North King is hunting her and he will not stop until she is caught . . .'

As Kallie finished, she was surprised to see everyone was clapping and cheering. Even Marlow clapped a few times, not wanting to be left out. Kallie's spirits soared, her worries about the quill far behind her. She felt a swoop of joy. And in that moment, she could hardly dare believe how lucky she was to be there, at Wildstorm, with people who loved stories and theatre as much as she did.

But then she noticed that Jackie was the only person who hadn't applauded. Kallie couldn't understand the expression on her face: the director's eyes were narrowed in disappointment.

CHAPTER SEVEN

At morning break – or 'biscuits and squash', as Violet called it – the cast trooped back to Hollowstar House. The tables were crammed with plates of chocolate bourbons, custard creams, jammy double-deckers – all handmade from the Marmalade Café – alongside jugs of orange squash and a giant pot of tea. The heat washed over them, and the surrounding meadows shone as if a giant paintbrush had just glided across the landscape. Tiny blue-winged birds zigzagged over the lawn and the flowers vibrated with bees.

Kallie and Emilia were still laughing about Emilia's speech, which had been about a crow called Crow.

'It was the only name I could think of!' Emilia chortled. 'I'm so bad at making things up. Luckily I want to be an actress – I'll leave the writing to the real playwrights. I dunno how you do it. Can I have a read of your speech?'

Emilia reached over the table for Kallie's notebook.

'Oh no! It's so messy,' protested Kallie, pulling the notebook out of reach.

A hot blush crept up her face. She didn't let anyone read her writing apart from her mum.

'You can read mine,' said Emilia. 'I drew the crow and it looks like a banana with legs. Look.'

But Kallie's hands were glued to her notebook.

'No. It's just . . . I'm bad at spelling and sometimes I write the wrong word and it doesn't make sense.' Kallie squirmed. 'And I have funny handwriting. And . . .' Her voice dropped so no one around them could hear her. 'And . . . I'm – I'm like . . . I'm dyslexic.'

Kallie felt her face burn. She waited for Emilia's expression to change, for her to realise that her new friend was in fact one of those stupid 'bottom set' kids who had extra lessons during lunch break. But Emilia's face didn't change. In fact, she let out a wild laugh.

'Pahaha! What does that matter?' She snorted. 'You're the Wildstorm playwriting winner! Writing isn't about being the best speller! It's about the best ideas – the best stories! Who cares about spelling when you're taking people on an adventure?'

Kallie had never thought about it like that before.

'I guess . . .' She gave a small smile. 'I guess that's what I love about the theatre – no one can see how bad your spelling is, they just watch your story onstage. Does that sound stupid?'

'Not at all.' Emilia grinned. 'You know what! Let's go on a real adventure at lunchtime – you might get some more ideas.'

There was a look of mischief in Emilia's eye. Kallie hesitated. Just being at Wildstorm was already an adventure for her. But she didn't want to admit this to Emilia.

'Sure!' she said and, with a deep breath, she handed over her notebook. 'I'm in.'

The Wildstormers returned to the meadow after break and Violet ran a workshop on making up characters: they used the props and took it in turns to be interviewed in groups. Kallie and Emilia partnered together and became elderly Elizabethan explorers who were always bickering about who'd discovered the potato first.

When lunch was announced, Emilia gave Kallie a knowing nod and slipped out of sight in the crowd. Five minutes later, Kallie ducked out of the lunch queue and hurried around the side of Hollowstar House. She wove her way through the trees towards the theatre, her heart pounding. Emilia was waiting there, waving a huge brass key.

'Swiped it from Mum's bedroom!' Emilia grinned. 'I know it's a risk but you've *got* to see the theatre before everyone else – it's incredible!'

'All right.' Kallie nodded. 'But if we get caught—'

'I'll say it was all my idea, I promise!'

Kallie knew they were breaking one of Jackie's three rules but the lure of the empty theatre was too good an adventure to ignore. Kallie was far from a rule-breaker at school but surely there was no harm in exploring a little. She held her breath as Emilia turned the key in the lock and the double doors creaked open.

The theatre was silent as a sleeping giant. It was shaped like a hexagon, six white walls with six high windows hung with black curtains. Black wooden beams arched over their heads, like the ribs of a beast. But Kallie's eyes were drawn to the stage. The stage. It was small but with just enough room for twenty kids to squeeze on together, set back under a proscenium arch, which led off to a backstage area on either side. At the back was a plain canvas sheet, ready to be brought to life with shapes and colours. A block of three-tiered steps was placed in front of the stage so the actors could walk up on to the stage from the auditorium.

It wasn't hard to imagine that a curse lay heavy over the place. Kallie could almost smell the mystery hanging in the air. It was as if the theatre was watching them closely, waiting to see how they would use it.

'What are those markings?' asked Kallie, her voice echoing.

They were the same strange symbols from Hollowstar House, etched into the beams and around the window frames: circular flower-like patterns.

'Witch's marks,' said Emilia, with relish. 'All part of the Ellsabet Graveheart curse, so the villagers say.'

Emilia scrambled on to the stage and Kallie followed.

'It's only got one backdrop,' said Emilia. 'It's not big enough to do fancy set changes but that doesn't matter. It was built in 1600, you know, Elizabethan times. Every owner has added something new to the theatre. The new roof was put in about two hundred years ago; it used to be thatched before – but it kept catching fire. But no one has actually put on a play here in four hundred years – we're the first.'

'How come?' asked Kallie.

'The other owners wanted to do plays but they kept having problems.' Emilia shrugged. 'Bad luck. It's been all shut up for ages – until Mum inherited it from Great-Aunt Meryl. It's taken ages to get it all fixed up.'

'I can't believe it's still here,' said Kallie, her voice hushed, 'after all this time.'

'There used to be a balcony above the stage, but it rotted away years ago,' said Emilia. 'And look at this!'

Emilia stepped into the wings – the sides of the stage, which were hidden from the audience. Kallie followed and saw a series of levers and dials on the wall; there were ropes connected to the rigging above them. Emilia pointed at the levers.

'These open the trap doors,' she explained. 'I begged Mum to put them in!'

Kallie looked back at the wooden stage floor and saw the faint outlines of three squares: secret trapdoors ready to fly open.

'And down there is the costume cupboard,' said Emilia, pointing to a door backstage. 'That's where last year's Wildstorm props get stored.'

'Like that green quill?' said Kallie, jumping on the subject. 'Do you know where it came from?'

'Oh, that. Yeah, it's from the house. Mum keeps it in a jar in her bedroom usually.'

Kallie held her breath. There was no way she would have seen it when she'd walked through Hollowstar House last night. So how had the quill ended up in her dream?

'Where did your mum get—'

There was a bang and they both froze.

'I think I forgot to close the door,' whispered Emilia, going pale.

'Keep back,' breathed Kallie and they both shrank against the backstage wall.

Kallie's throat went dry. What would Jackie do if she found them? Would she kick Kallie out of the camp? For a second there was silence and then they heard the unmistakable sound of footsteps. Someone was moving stealthily towards the stage.

'Can you see who it is?' Emilia mouthed and Kallie shook her head.

Her heart racing, Kallie ducked low and crept forward so she could peer into the auditorium.

It wasn't Jackie or any of the staff. Someone else was creeping across the floor. It was a boy she didn't recognise and she knew at once that he shouldn't be there.

He was looking around but then his eyes focused on something on the stage. A rucksack that had been pushed into a corner. The boy stole across the floor and climbed up on to the boards.

Suddenly Kallie had an idea. Without a moment to lose, she dived at one of the levers on the wall and

pulled it – Emilia cried out in shock – so did the boy!
A trapdoor had opened below him but Kallie had pulled
the lever too late. One of the boy's feet had fallen
through the hole but he was quickly scrambling upright.

The boy lunged at the rucksack but Emilia had leapt
on to the stage and she and the boy both seized it at
the same time. Kallie clattered up behind Emilia and
grabbed hold of the bag too. She locked eyes with the
boy and was shocked to see the unnaturally blank
expression on his face—

'Let go! You thieving pig!' yelled Emilia.

The boy was losing his grip – his arms strained and
for a second Kallie's eye was drawn to something
on the boy's wrist. It was the letter C in black ink.
She leant forward but before she could take a closer
look, the bag flew out of the boy's hands and into
Emilia's lap – it burst open, blinding them in a blizzard
of papers.

The boy turned tail and pelted for the theatre doors.
He was gone before they could follow.

'What's all this?' Kallie gasped, picking up the sheets
of paper.

'It's Mum's rucksack,' panted Emilia, 'she must have
left it here. Hey! Look at this!'

She was holding one of the papers. It was cracked

and curling at the edges and with a sudden thrill Kallie realised exactly what it was: it was a playscript. The Wildstorm play.

And then Kallie noticed the title and her stomach clenched.

The King's Downfall
by Ellsabet Graveheart

Ellsabet. The witch.

CHAPTER EIGHT

There were whispers of wonder as the Wildstormers filed into the theatre after lunch. Kallie felt the theatre vibrate as their collective voices floated up towards the high hexagonal ceiling.

Kallie and Emilia hung back as everyone grabbed a chair from the side. They had gathered up the script, put it all back in the rucksack and Emilia had managed to put the key back in Hollowstar House before lunch had finished. Under the cover of the clattering and scraping of chairs, Kallie turned to Emilia.

'Did you know Ellsabet was a playwright?' said Kallie.

Unease was simmering in her stomach. The idea of a local witch had seemed exciting at first but seeing Ellsabet Graveheart's name on that script had been like watching a villain step off the stage and into the real world.

'No,' Emilia muttered back, 'I thought she cursed

the theatre to *stop* people having fun here. Didn't realise she wrote a play.'

'And why did the boy want to steal it?' pressed Kallie. 'Who was he?'

'Some village kid. I think I've seen him before. Told you they were snoops.'

'Do the villagers know about Ellsabet's play?' wondered Kallie.

'Can't see how they would,' said Emilia. 'He was probably just nosing around – took a chance when he saw the doors were open.' Emilia pulled an angry face. 'You know, I bet Mr Mildew put him up to it.'

'The head of the Historical Society? Why?'

'Probably looking for an excuse to get the show cancelled' – Emilia sniffed – 'and get Mum in trouble.'

Violet called for quiet and they both hurried to sit down. Jackie swept between the chairs and up to the stage. Kallie still wasn't sure what to make of Emilia's mum. She hadn't liked Kallie's speech, that had been clear. Perhaps it had been something to do with the quill, Kallie wondered. Jackie's calculating eyes always seemed to settle on her, as if she was looking for an answer she couldn't quite find.

'This year's Wildstorm play has never been performed before,' announced Jackie, her voice ringing through the theatre. 'It was written over four hundred years ago by a woman who lived here in Merricombe. Ellsabet Graveheart.'

A murmur washed through the cast. Kallie could see that many of them recognised the name, while others, like new Wildstormer, Ivan, looked simply confused.

'Those of you who live in Merricombe might think that Ellsabet was a witch. This is a nonsense tale made up by pea-brained twits.' Jackie glared around at them as if daring someone to contradict her. '*The King's Downfall*,' she continued, 'is an epic battle between good and evil.' She held up the old manuscript for them all to see. 'Some small parts of the script have been lost over the years but we shall use what we have. This play was written to be performed in this theatre and I am honoured that we have a chance to bring it to life. Tomorrow we will read the play and I shall hand out the parts but for now can I have a volunteer to read the narrator's opening speech?'

Unsurprisingly, it was Marlow's hand that shot up first. Kallie was perfectly happy not to be reading aloud. Marlow took the script, climbed up on to the stage and began to read:

'Join us, oh merry friends, as players now unveil

A plot of hope and fear: the storyteller's tale.

Our heroine, she uses words to warm the coldest soul.

She's fled the cruel North King, for freedom is her goal.

He's full of loathing for her tales, hates the good they make;

Her stories calm the fearful, make brave those who quake.'

Kallie felt shock flood her insides like cold water. It couldn't be . . . Marlow paused and looked directly at her. People were starting to whisper as Marlow read on, a slight smirk on his face:

'The Southern Lord gives shelter from her dreadful foe

But behind her comes the King, cloaked in storms of woe.

49

> The King is power-mad; he will not let her win,
>
> So listen close and listen hard, and let our play begin.'

Everyone was staring at Kallie. Even Emilia.

'Looks like wonder girl is just a sneaky copycat after all,' hissed Marlow, as he sat down amongst his friends.

Kallie felt breathless. She dared not look at Emilia. She didn't want to see Emilia's expression of disappointment and pity. She didn't want to look at anybody.

Jackie was talking again but Kallie wasn't listening.

The speech – some of it word for word – was exactly the same as the story she had written that morning: the story inspired by the quill. How was that possible? Panic was rising inside her. She'd never heard of Ellsabet Graveheart before today and apparently the plot to Ellsabet's play was already inside Kallie's head! It didn't make any sense.

Kallie felt like she was trapped in a nightmare. After the speech, Ray, the set designer, had given a talk on theatre safety and they divided into groups for an improvisation game. When the last group had performed, there was a scrum at the theatre door, as people rushed to be first in the queue for dinner. Kallie drifted behind everyone in a daze.

Emilia had been called away to speak to Jackie, so Kallie walked down to Hollowstar House alone, trying to ignore the stares all around her. The sunny optimism she'd been feeling about the week was a distant memory. She couldn't work it out. How on earth had this happened?

Dinner was piping-hot jacket potatoes with spicy bean chilli. Smudge was winding around Burn's legs; the cat was the only creature the cook seemed to like. Kallie hoped she was imagining the look of judgement in Smudge's green eyes.

'If you ask me, I'd say she cheated at the playwriting competition too.' Marlow's voice hissed behind her. 'How do we know she didn't copy it from someone else?'

Kallie took her plate to the furthest end of the table; those sitting nearest shuffled away from her and she hung her head, wishing she was invisible. No one was going to believe she wasn't a cheat. It was clear she didn't belong at Wildstorm after all.

'There you are! Orange squash?'

Emilia slid on to the bench opposite her.

'I managed to convince Mum we haven't been sneaking around the theatre – so we're in the clear,' said Emilia, tucking into her potato. 'What's up?'

'Um . . .' Kallie stared wildly at her. 'Um . . . the speech?'

'Oh, that!' Emilia shrugged. 'That was weird, wasn't it? What a freaky coincidence!'

'You . . . you don't think I'm a lying copycat?' Kallie stammered.

Emilia gave her a baffled look. 'Mate, if you'd seen your face! I know you were just as surprised as the rest of us.'

Kallie was so grateful, she couldn't speak for a whole minute.

'Honestly, I've never seen the script before,' Kallie said weakly. 'I've got no idea what happened. This morning – it was like the story had been planted in my mind.'

It sounded a bit dramatic when she said it out loud and Emilia stared at her.

'You think someone . . . ?' Emilia mimed plucking something from thin air and putting it in Kallie's head. 'I'm sure it was a coincidence – or maybe like a subconscious thing.'

'But I'd never even heard of Ellsabet Graveheart before today and your mum said this is the first time the play has been performed.'

There was an edge of panic in Kallie's voice now.

'Well, there must be a reason. We'll work it out,' said Emilia comfortingly.

Kallie slumped over her potato, feeling hopeless.

'And there's another thing.' Kallie took a great breath. 'I . . . I didn't tell you earlier but that green quill . . . I saw it in my dream last night.' She squinted up at Emilia. 'The quill must be connected to Ellsabet, right? She was a playwright after all. Maybe I've caught the curse?'

Emilia burst out laughing. 'What, like a cold?' She pointed at Kallie with a forkful of chilli. 'You are not cursed. Look, you came last night, you must have seen the play and the quill in Hollowstar House. And it just stuck in your imagination.'

'That's what I thought at first but . . .'

Any logical solution sounded more and more unlikely.

'Chin up!' Emilia gave a potatoey smile. 'At least Mum doesn't know we snuck into the theatre.'

Kallie was struck by a thought. 'Hey, you know that boy in the theatre, did you see the mark on his wrist?'

'No,' Emilia said.

'It was like a tattoo. In the shape of a C.'

'Brownie points to any kid who can get a tattoo without their parents going ballistic!' Emilia laughed. 'It was probably just a weird spot.'

'Maybe . . .'

Emilia tried to cheer Kallie up by building a pyramid with the cups on the table – much to the annoyance of those still drinking out of them.

The jacket potatoes were followed by warm apple tart, whipped cream and hot chocolate. Kallie and Emilia remained sitting at the table until the sky had turned navy and the fairy lights were glittering in the garden. But Kallie couldn't shake off the feeling of unease: it felt like someone was playing a trick on her. At least she had Emilia on her side. She'd never really had a best friend before – not that she was calling Emilia her best friend after one day of knowing her – but talking to Emilia was so easy and familiar.

'So if your mum inherited Hollowstar House from your great-aunt, then do you live here now?' said Kallie, as they took their empty bowls back to the kitchen.

'No. We only stay here in the summer and when Mum's working on the theatre,' said Emilia, looking up at the house fondly. 'We live in Bristol most of the time – that's where I go to school and Mum's got her theatre company. Smudge doesn't mind moving around. Lots of us are from Bristol or nearby.'

'Still hanging around with the copycat, are you, Em?' Marlow had sauntered over from the tables, his giggling friends like a cloud of midges around him. Ivan was trailing behind them, eager to be involved.

Emilia folded her arms. Kallie tried to look unconcerned, but she could feel her face going pink.

'Kallie isn't a copycat,' snarled Emilia.

'Sure,' sniggered Marlow, 'I knew there was something weird about you. Asking all these questions about Ellsabet Graveheart when you already knew the answers.'

'So what do you know about Ellsabet Graveheart, then?' said Kallie.

'Well, you might learn a thing or two about old Ellsabet at the Wildstorm Challenge tonight.'

'Challenge?' squeaked Ivan. 'What – what challenge?'

'The challenge is a tradition every new Stormer must face before becoming a true member of the cast.' Marlow grinned.

Kallie's heart dropped.

'Pah! What nonsense!' snorted Emilia. 'I've never heard of this! It's not a *thing*.'

'Well, I've just started it,' said Marlow, reddening.

'So it's not a tradition—'

'Whatever!' Marlow tossed his head, and his eyes snapped back to Kallie. 'We're meeting at midnight by the hut. I hope you're not afraid of the dark . . .'

He turned on his heel and left, his friends chattering behind him.

'Oh, Marlow's talking rubbish.' Emilia rolled her eyes. 'You don't need to go to any challenge – you're already a Wildstormer.'

'Am I?' sighed Kallie, before she could stop herself. 'Maybe I don't have a choice.'

A slow resolve was growing in Kallie's stomach. She looked down to the campsite, watching the purple shadows bleeding out over the lawn. If this challenge was the price she had to pay to find out about Ellsabet and become a real Wildstormer, then so be it.

CHAPTER NINE

The night was warm and cloudless. Zipped up in her sleeping bag, Kallie listened to the rumble of conversations from the tents around her. She knew everyone was whispering about her – the strange new girl who had tried to pass off the play for her own. The liar who'd cheated to win her place at Wildstorm.

Kallie reached for her notebook; it would be a while until she could sleep, that was for sure. Emilia slept in Hollowstar House and Kallie had returned to the campsite alone. She'd gone straight into her tent, while everyone else sat around the meadow, talking and laughing.

Kallie lay back, looking up at the colourful lights on the ceiling and felt safe inside her cosy cocoon. She hadn't bothered changing into her pyjamas. She was fully dressed, ready for her midnight appointment with Marlow and the Wildstorm Challenge.

Did she really think the theatre curse was real? Every

time Ellsabet Graveheart's name was mentioned, Kallie felt a shiver creep down her spine. She had always hoped she'd feel brave when faced with a real mystery, like the characters she wrote about in her plays. But instead she felt muddled and panicked.

Her pen was in her hand and she found herself writing:

I may not be a hero, but I am braver than you think.

It was a pretty good line. If only she believed it. She'd have to use it in a play one day. Maybe Emilia could act in it.

Writing always helped Kallie feel calmer: her imagination was like a warm blanket, keeping out the cold world. Soon she was drifting to sleep, thoughts of witches and curses darkening her dreams.

Hours later, Kallie woke with a start, her phone alarm beeping in her ear. She fumbled to turn it off. It was silent outside. Without turning her torch on, Kallie found her trainers and slowly unzipped the tent.

Everything was still under the grey moonless sky. Kallie tiptoed through the tents, holding her breath as she circled the staff tent. Her heart was hitting her ribs. The cry of a fox rang out over the meadows and she jumped wildly. She reached the bathroom hut, feeling shaken. The light was on inside the hut, and she stood near the doorway, looking around into the black shadows. What if this was a set-up? What if Marlow was planning to trick her?

Then she heard footsteps and four figures emerged from the darkness: Marlow, two of his friends and a terrified-looking Ivan.

'It's the wannabe playwright, out all alone,' Marlow sing-songed. 'Think you're brave enough for the Wildstorm Challenge?'

'I'm here, aren't I?' said Kallie, as strongly as she could. 'Let's get this over with.'

'Hear, hear!' came a voice from behind Kallie, as Emilia stepped into the light.

'The challenge is for new Stormers!' growled Marlow.

'Sabina and Tilly aren't new.' Emilia pointed to his friends. 'I just want to learn about this long, ancient tradition you've started!'

'OK!' Marlow hissed. 'But keep your voice down. We don't want to get caught.'

Kallie grinned at Emilia, her nerves momentarily forgotten. Her friend gave her an innocent shrug.

'Couldn't let you have all the fun,' Emilia whispered.

They set off, feeling their way around the edge of

the meadow. Torches off. They tramped through the field beyond the campsite, no one speaking. And as they reached the edge of the wood, Marlow turned to face them and flicked on his torch; he held it under his chin so his cheekbones stood out spookily.

'The Wildstorm Challenge starts here,' he announced. 'A tradition all Wildstormers must face. To walk in the footsteps of the witch Ellsabet Graveheart—'

'I just hope we're the same shoe size,' muttered Emilia. 'People had smaller feet four hundred years ago.'

Kallie laughed; even one of Marlow's friends tittered.

'If you're going to mess around, then don't come!' snapped Marlow. 'I've forgotten the rest of my speech now,' he grumbled. 'Anyway – we're going this way. Let the new Stormers be blindfolded!'

'No thanks,' gulped Kallie.

'I'll fall over!' stuttered Ivan. 'Dad says I have innate clumsiness; it's a family characteristic . . .'

'OK, forget the blindfolds,' huffed Marlow. 'Let's just go.'

They trekked uphill through the trees, Emilia grinning as if it was all a jolly outing. Kallie was glad she was there but she couldn't relax. She felt a prickling feeling on the back of her neck as they roamed deeper into the woodland. Poor Ivan was stumbling over the uneven ground. Kallie had to grab his arm to stop him falling face forward into a muddy brook. Over Ivan's puffing, Kallie was aware of the trees shifting around them. The darkness was playing tricks with her eyes, the blackness looming into monstrous shapes, which seeped away like ink before she could panic. There was a bad feeling in the wood. Kallie didn't feel remotely brave; she just wished Marlow's game would be finished soon.

But then – just as they climbed up a particularly steep slope, Kallie heard something. A low growl on the wind. Maybe it *was* the wind. It sounded like a word, just out of earshot. She stumbled to a stop.

'What's up?' whispered Emilia, pointing her torch into the surrounding trees.

'Nothing . . . just noises.'

The darkness lifted slightly as they left the wood and the ground changed from dry leaves to dusty grass. They were nearing the top of the hill. And with the trees behind them, the night sky opened up like a dome: navy and purple with stars brighter than Kallie had ever seen. There was enough grey light to show the faces of the others.

'This is Fallow Hill,' said Emilia proudly. 'The most beautiful spot in Gloucestershire.'

Looking around, Kallie knew that, on a bright day, you'd be able to see for miles in every direction. But that night, the ghostly landscape below them was a quilt of grey, silver and charcoal meadows.

At the very top of the hill, the ground flattened out like a tabletop. There was a cluster of trees, tall and slender, standing in a circle, surrounding a rugged old tree stump.

The hairs on Kallie's arms stood up. She clutched Emilia's elbow.

'I've – I know this place,' Kallie whispered. 'In my dream, this is where I saw the quill.'

For the first time, Emilia looked scared. Kallie gripped her own torch and stared around the hilltop, her heart beating painfully.

'Behold Ellsabet the Witch!' announced Marlow, and with a flourish he produced a piece of fabric.

He unrolled it to reveal a picture. Ellsabet the Witch glared out at Kallie. The artist had given her a face like a skull, two black eyes and bedraggled weeds of hair. Kallie's skin crawled as Ellsabet's eyes seemed to flash in the torchlight.

'Is that a tea towel?' said Emilia, breaking the silence.

'Oh, shut up!' shot Marlow. He stuffed it back into his pocket and spread his arms wide. 'And further behold the great blackthorn stump! Where the evil Ellsabet was burnt for witchcraft. Ellsabet Graveheart was a stranger in Merricombe and the villagers didn't like strangers. She arrived dressed in rags and begged a local landlord to give her shelter. He let Ellsabet into his home – but little did he know, she was as rotten as bad eggs!' Marlow grinned, pleased with his simile. 'Strange things started happening to the villagers of Merricombe: children got sick, food turned bad, a great drought starved the villagers. It was all Ellsabet's doing. She even used her evil magic to enchant the landlord's son, John Graveheart, into marrying her and used him as her servant.'

Kallie's throat was dry. She knew Marlow was just trying to scare them but her mind was racing at his words. If Ellsabet had really had powers to enchant people, would she also have the power to plant stories in people's heads? To give her victims bad dreams? But this was four hundred years ago, Kallie reminded herself; Ellsabet was long gone.

'At last, the villagers had had enough,' continued Marlow. 'They stormed Ellsabet's cottage with pitchforks and burning stakes and marched her to the top of Fallow Hill, where she was tried for witchcraft and found guilty. Now all new Stormers must do the

Wildstorm Challenge to protect themselves from the witch's curse.'

Beside Kallie, Ivan's teeth were chattering with fear.

'New Stormers,' Marlow cried, his voice echoing around the clearing, 'you will walk once around the blackthorn stump, saying "I will always be a Stormer; I will always be of Wildstorm". Then strike a match.'

'That's it?' scoffed Emilia. 'No funny dance? No climbing the tallest tree or eating a poisoned berry?'

'Don't give him ideas,' squealed Ivan.

'You're not even supposed to be here,' Marlow shot at Emilia. 'Stop being annoying. Everyone, turn off your torches. Ivan, you go first.'

Marlow thrust a box of matches into Ivan's hands.

With their torches off, the darkness closed in again. Kallie watched Ivan's silhouette walk around the stump, her heart beating hard. The tall trees surrounding them were creeping with shadows.

'I will always be a Stormer; I will always be of Wildstorm.' Ivan choked up the words.

He lit his match and the flame quivered.

'It's your go, genius.' Marlow handed the matchbox to Kallie. 'This should be easy – you just need to copy what someone else has done.'

Kallie hardly heard him; she was too focused on

the noises around them. That bad feeling was back. She took the matches and began to walk around the tree stump.

'I will always be a Stormer,' she recited. 'I will always be of—'

Her head jerked up. It was the growling noise again. This time she heard the word on the wind. *Ellsabet* . . . Had the others heard it too? It was so dark she could barely see them. She fumbled with the box of matches. Her heart was beating faster and faster. She struck a match.

The flame burst into life and Kallie saw him – standing right behind Emilia. Kallie screamed but the boy – a stranger – had grabbed Emilia and pulled her backwards into the darkness.

'Emilia!'

The match died as Kallie launched forward, groping blindly for her friend. Around them, the trees were full of voices – not just the confused shouts of the Wildstormers, but different voices all chanting the same word: 'Ellsabet . . . Ellsabet . . .'

Figures were closing in around them. Still flailing around in the darkness, Kallie stumbled over something hard – Emilia's torch. She dived for it and clicked it on. The beam found Emilia struggling with the boy; he was tugging at her jacket pocket. Without thinking, Kallie charged him, her shoulder colliding with his stomach, and he fell hard on the ground. Kallie flashed the torch in his face.

'Who are you and what do you want?' shouted Kallie, fear racing through her veins.

The boy stared up at her, his eyes oddly blank and opaque. There was a dark smudge on his wrist.

'Give us the keys,' the boy croaked.

'What? Why?'

'Ellsabet,' he mumbled and his comrades answered him.

'Ellsabet . . . Ellsabet . . . Ellsabet . . .'

Kallie darted the torch around the clearing; there were three boys in total, including the boy who'd broken into the theatre.

'The key to the theatre,' panted Emilia, still slumped on the ground. 'I haven't got it any more.'

The effect was instantaneous. The boy on the ground struggled to his feet and backed away into the trees. The other boys retreated too, their footsteps stumbling down the hill and vanishing into the night.

To Kallie's surprise, Emilia jumped up and was about to follow them. Kallie caught her arm and Emilia spun around; she had tears in her eyes.

'It was Arley,' cried Emilia, as Marlow and the others hurried up to them. 'H—he was at Wildstorm last year. He was my friend and h—he didn't even recognise me.'

Chapter Ten

Two fierce eyes glowed from behind a tree – watching the chaos on Fallow Hill.

The key was not there but the shadow had spotted something else. Something much more interesting. The girl. This was a great find indeed. Everything was falling into place: the reason it had returned.

She didn't look like much. But all children looked the same to the shadow. More robust than adults but still plain and simple in the shadow's eyes. But this one . . . she must be the one! There was no question about it. The shadow recognised that look of sickening defiance in the girl's face – anger boiled up like a poison. The girl was one thing but her friend looked like trouble. Friends were always trouble, in the shadow's experience, too loyal and too meddling.

The shadow darted through the darkness, wafting from tree to tree. Watching the drama with glee. It had been amusing at first – seeing the children parading around that old tree stump, telling stories and saying nonsense words. The shadow did enjoy a bit of nonsense. Oh, how the children howled deliciously when the unexpected visitors arrived! It was most entertaining.

It was a shame about the key – but this new discovery had chased away all thoughts of idle fun. There would be another way into the theatre; even in this weakened state, the shadow would manage it.

The children had gathered together, flashing their torches through the trees, speaking in panicked shrieks. Their fear heavy in the air. The shadow slithered closer, catching their voices . . .

'We should go . . .'

'. . . this was your idea, Marlow!'

'I've lost my torch . . .'

'Has anyone seen Ivan's torch?'

The shadow watched hungrily, bright eyes lingering on every face, looking for weaknesses.

A new plan was beginning to take shape. Yes . . . the shadow was strong enough to play another little trick. It was time to spread a little more fear. The shadow could handle the girl – and her friend too. There was much work to be done.

CHAPTER ELEVEN

Tuesday's breakfast was sausage and egg sandwiches with tomato ketchup. Kallie's vegetarian sausages were a special homemade invention from Burn made of mushrooms and red onions, which smelt delicious. Kallie and Emilia took their sandwiches and mugs of tea to the furthest table in the garden.

The morning sun illuminated spots of dew on the lawn and the canopy over the tables. Jackie's countdown fluttered on the kitchen door. It now read: *4 DAYS TO GO*.

Kallie's eyes were heavy with tiredness. After their midnight trek up and down Fallow Hill, she'd collapsed into another uneasy sleep. She couldn't shift the feeling that someone had been watching them on the hilltop, someone other than the three village boys.

As they ate breakfast, Emilia told Kallie about Arley. He lived in Merricombe and had been one of the first locals to sign up for Wildstorm the previous year.

He was a brilliant actor, he could play funny or serious, and by the final performance, Emilia and Arley had been firm friends. They used to make up songs together to help learn their lines and secretly try on the costumes at lunchtime. He had been looking forward to this year's show, but then, a few weeks before the camp was about to start, Arley stopped replying to Emilia's messages.

'That's when I had a look at the applications,' muttered Emilia, eyes down. 'And saw he wasn't coming back this year.' She took a sad bite of her sandwich. 'I know his dad thinks theatre is a waste of time – but Arley could have said something to me. I haven't heard from him in weeks.'

'Maybe he was upset he couldn't come,' suggested Kallie, 'and didn't know how to tell you.'

'Maybe he just doesn't want to know me any more,' mumbled Emilia.

Kallie sipped her tea in sympathetic silence. Fellow Wildstormers were hovering around the kitchen door, hoping for seconds, Smudge meowing around their ankles.

'Did you see the tattoo on Arley's wrist?' asked Kallie. Emilia shook her head. 'Do you think he's joined some kind of gang?'

'A gang in Merricombe?' Emilia gave a weak laugh. 'Not likely . . .'

'It was similar to the one the other boy had,' muttered Kallie, 'a C – but thicker than the other boy's tattoo – or whatever they are. What do you think C stands for?'

'No idea,' sighed Emilia, clearly still thinking about Arley. 'I just don't know why he'd do something like that. The Arley I knew wouldn't play a stupid prank.'

It hadn't felt like a prank to Kallie. She knew what she'd seen last night – the boys moving in that odd way, like moths drawn to a bright light. There had been a word on the wind, a word they had been chanting . . . *Ellsabet* . . . But in the light of day, it was as if Emilia had forgotten the strangeness of the night before.

'But why wouldn't Arley recognise you?' said Kallie softly.

'He's probably embarrassed he ever came to Wildstorm,' mumbled Emilia, 'so of course he'd pretend not to know me.'

Kallie hated seeing Emilia so sombre. She cut off half her sandwich and offered to it Emilia, who took it with watery-eyed thanks. Kallie was already starting to realise that food was a good way of making

Emilia happy. Over her head, Kallie saw Marlow heading towards their table. He plonked his plate next to Emilia.

'You should have seen your faces last night,' he said. 'What a pair of scaredy-cats.'

'I'd rather be a scaredy-cat than a crybaby,' retorted Emilia. 'I heard you snivelling all the way back.'

'If you hadn't tagged along we wouldn't have had to deal with those idiots,' tutted Marlow.

'What do you mean?' said Kallie.

'You saw them – Emilia was the one they wanted to scare. Ruined my Wildstorm Challenge; I didn't even get to do the ending,' he sulked. 'You had to eat a whole chocolate bar while standing on one leg.'

'You had chocolate and you didn't give us any?!' cried Emilia.

But Kallie was turning over what he'd just said. It was true the boys had gone straight to Emilia but surely that was because they'd been looking for the key to the theatre? Or had they actually just been aiming to scare her? Were they still after the script? Or was Emilia herself their target?

'So what do you think the village boys wanted?' said Kallie to Marlow.

'They wanted to kidnap Emilia and burn her like

the witch,' teased Marlow. 'Didn't you hear what they were whispering?'

'You – you heard it too?' Kallie was taken aback.

'"Ellsabet" – that's what they were saying.' Marlow nodded.

'Well, I didn't hear anything,' scoffed Emilia, picking up her empty plate. 'Come on, Kallie. Let's go.'

Kallie followed Emilia to the kitchen. She didn't know what to make of it. They'd both heard the whispering but Emilia hadn't. At least that meant it wasn't all in her imagination. But she wasn't sure if that was a comfort or not.

Burn was throwing out sausage ends for Smudge, and Kallie bent to give the cat a good-morning scratch. There was a commotion behind them and Kallie looked up to see Jackie come bursting from Hollowstar House, a grim expression on her face. Jackie marched off in the direction of the theatre and Kallie caught Emilia's eye; with a nod, they followed curiously after the director. They weren't the only ones. Ahead, some of the cast were already congregating outside the theatre, voices hushed and panicked.

As they drew closer, Kallie saw a small group of strangers – villagers, she supposed – all clustering around the theatre doors. Every face was stern and unsmiling. Kallie felt the hairs on her neck begin to prickle.

'What's going on?' said Emilia, stopping Marlow's friend Sab.

'It's a mess.' Sabina shuddered. 'They don't know who did it.'

Kallie craned her neck to see over the crowd. Splashed across the doors to the theatre, written in white paint, were the words:

THIS THEATRE IS CURSED

Kallie felt a wave of dread. Beside her, Emilia gasped angrily.

'Did I not predict this outcome?' A pompous voice rang out, silencing the crowd. 'Did I not warn you?'

A man was standing in the centre of a group of villagers, leaning on an elegant cane. He was tall and willowy with thinning grey hair. His voice was soft and sly, but it had a way of capturing your attention.

'We knew it would end badly,' the man continued, 'opening the theatre and bringing youths into our village. And now this: vandalism of a historical property!'

'That's Mr Mildew,' whispered Emilia, 'head of the Historical Society.'

'My cast had nothing to do with this!' Jackie was standing at the front of the theatre group, her eyes blazing. 'We can't be blamed for—'

'Merricombe deserves more respect,' Mr Mildew carried on as if no one had spoken. 'Clearly these children are not old enough to appreciate historical importance.'

'We have not broken any laws, Mr Mildew.' Jackie scowled. 'This silliness is clearly the work of a few bored village kids! I have done everything the Historical Society has advised but you have no business sticking your nose into what goes on in my theatre,' Jackie puffed, extending to her fullest height.

'The theatre is a historical building, whether you own it or not. It is naturally the business of the society,' said Mr Mildew, his tone sickly sweet. 'And now I have received a note telling me that you are in possession of an important historical document. A script by Ellsabet the Witch – that script needs to be in the safe hands of the society, along with all items relating to the witch.'

Kallie's ears pricked up.

'The society has no legal power to demand historical items from those who discovered them,' said Violet at Jackie's side.

'No, but we have a duty – a duty to history,' said Mr Mildew, and the villagers around him nodded in agreement.

Jackie scowled.

'Disturbing the theatre is bad enough,' Mr Mildew went on, 'but since your theatre kids arrived there's been some very nasty goings-on in the village. There has been a break-in at the Historical Society office! Our safety is under threat. Perhaps it is not wise for the Wildstorm performance to go ahead this year.'

'My cast have better things to do than go poking around the Historical Society office,' Jackie snorted. 'I could not think of a more boring place to burgle!'

The cast behind her sniggered and Mr Mildew's face turned stormy.

'Do you refuse to hand over the script for historical examination?'

'At last, you understand me. You're not taking the script,' concluded Jackie. '*The King's Downfall* by Ellsabet Graveheart will be performed this Saturday, whether you like it or not. Now kindly leave – we have rehearsals to start.' And Jackie stalked back towards the house, calling behind her: 'Wildstormers, assemble in the theatre in ten minutes. Don't be late!'

For their first task that day, the cast broke into groups and were told to make up an interesting way of performing the narrator's opening speech. Kallie and Emilia were teamed with Ivan; he still looked shellshocked from the night before and kept nibbling his fingernails nervously. The morning was bright so the cast dispersed between the trees outside the theatre, some going as far as the garden so other groups didn't steal their ideas.

'Come on, this way.' Emilia gestured, leading Kallie and Ivan around the back of the theatre.

No one else was coming their way. Once they'd turned the corner, they were quite alone, dwarfed by the towering theatre on one side and the trees stretched out around them, their branches creating a canopy of quiet.

They started reading the speech again and thinking up a couple of ideas. But before they could get going, Ivan gasped that he needed his sun cream – he was looking rather flushed – and trotted off to find it.

'Do you think Ivan's going to be all right in the play?' said Kallie. 'He looks sick every time he gets near the stage.'

'He'll be fine!' Emilia turned to Kallie, as if picking up on a conversation they'd already started. 'So the

Historical Society know about the play.'

'But how did they find out? Mr Mildew said he got a note.'

'Must have been the snooping village boys,' growled Emilia.

'So does that mean the boys were working for Mr Mildew?' said Kallie. 'It still doesn't explain the C on their arms. What does it stand for? If only it was called the Historical *Club* – that would fit.'

'Yeah, but I can't see Mr Mildew giving out tattoos,' snorted Emilia.

'And why would the Historical Society want the village boys to chase us on Fallow Hill and write that message on the door? Mr Mildew seemed just as annoyed about that as your mum.'

'He was faking it. He's using the curse to get the villagers all scared so they help him shut down Wildstorm. I bet you he wrote that message about the curse himself.'

'But why? They were fine with Wildstorm last year,' said Kallie.

'Because Mr Mildew is a control freak!' tutted Emilia.

'But what if . . .' Kallie glanced instinctively around at the trees, checking they were alone. 'What if the boys aren't spying for Mr Mildew; what if they're working for someone else?'

'Who else is there?'

'I don't know.' Kallie didn't want to say Ellsabet Graveheart's name but it stuck in the back of her throat.

It was a ridiculous idea, of course. A witch from four hundred years ago, returned to cause havoc with the local theatre production. And yet . . . Kallie felt a shiver pass over her as she remembered the feeling of being watched from the night before.

She looked up at the theatre and saw more of the witch's marks, like faded circular flowers chiselled into the stone. The undergrowth grew close to the theatre wall here, vines creeping up the stone. Something caught Kallie's eye. She moved closer, pushing back the outer bushes; there was something dark beyond the brambles. In between the gnarled thorns, Kallie could just make out a small wooden door in the theatre wall.

Chapter Twelve

The door was set in a sunken archway in the theatre wall. It's cracked wood was so old and weather-beaten it had turned grey.

Kallie and Emilia waded through the undergrowth to get a closer look, ignoring the cuts and stings on their arms. Kallie pressed a hand against the door and felt the mottled wood.

'Do you know where this goes?' said Kallie softly; there was something about this door that made her want to talk in whispers.

'I've never noticed it before,' Emilia answered.

'Do you reckon we can open it?' Kallie gave it a tentative push; the door stayed stubbornly shut.

There was a lock, blackened with age, which they took turns rattling with no result. Kallie suddenly had an idea.

'Wait here!' she told Emilia, before slipping back through the undergrowth and running around the side of the theatre. Her stomach was fizzing with excitement. She needed to get inside that door – something told her that answers lay beyond it. Answers to the truth behind the curse or even a clue to the mysterious C.

A few minutes later, Kallie was hurrying back to Emilia, holding up the green quill. She'd swiped it from the crate of props when Violet's back had been turned. She approached the door and Emilia stepped back. Kallie pressed the tip of the quill into the lock and twisted it this way and that. Just when Kallie was about to give up hope, the lock clicked and the door creaked open. The two of them peered into the darkness.

'Wouldn't hurt to take a quick look,' said Kallie casually.

'It'll hurt if we slip and break our necks!' warned Emilia. 'Go slowly.'

Kallie glanced back at the trees. The wind was rustling through the leaves, making them whisper to each other.

'Let's go now, before anyone comes,' said Kallie.

Feeling her way into the darkness, Kallie descended down a flight of stone steps. She counted eight steps until she reached the bottom. The light from the door above barely illuminated an arm's reach around her but Kallie could make out something bulky in the darkness.

'I've got my pocket torch,' came Emilia's voice behind her.

A small beam of light shone over Kallie's shoulder. She gasped – for a horrible moment she thought the room was full of people – but they were costumes. Beautiful, bejewelled costumes arranged on mannequins in the dark corners and more costumes hanging on two rails. The small chamber had shelves built into the walls and they were piled high with hats, blooming with feathers. Everything was covered in dust, which glowed silver in the torchlight.

Kallie and Emilia moved forward, wary of straying too far from the stairway and the small pool of light from above. Kallie was trying not to look directly at the mannequins; they seemed eerily alive in the darkness.

'Are these costumes from old shows?' breathed Emilia.

'The shows they never got to perform,' added Kallie with wonder.

Now the shock was wearing off, Kallie found her curiosity mounting. A secret costume chamber hidden under a four-hundred-year-old theatre – who knew the treasures and stories that were hidden in this chamber?

'Shall we take a closer look?' Kallie suggested. Emilia nodded eagerly.

Kallie touched the nearest dress, the lace running through her fingers like grains of rice. The next hanger was a jacket and lace ruff; moths had eaten away half of the velvet, but it was no less impressive.

'How old do you reckon these are?' said Emilia, who was examining a shelf of glinting necklaces.

'It's hard to tell,' Kallie said, squinting around. 'Some things have almost rotted away but others are all right. And these hangers look newer. Looks like people have been adding to the collection for years.'

'I wonder if Mum knows about this,' muttered Emilia.

Something caught Kallie's eye and she squatted down next to a low shelf. There was an ancient chest, which glinted in the torchlight. Kallie dug her nails into the lid. It was heavy but she managed to prise it open. Her heart fluttered expectantly but the chest was empty.

Disappointed, Kallie moved back to the rack of costumes. She trailed her hand along the exquisite garments, wondering at their stories, but then she paused – there was a small hole in the hem of one of the dresses. Kallie bent down. She could feel something sewn inside the material. She pulled at the threads and eased out the item hidden inside: it was a wad of parchment. Before she could unroll it, a shadow blocked the light above them. Her head snapped up. She could see Emilia's outline on the other side of the chamber, her wide eyes suddenly alert.

Thump-thump. Someone was walking down the stairs. *Thump-thump.*

A shadow, bulky and lumbering, stretched towards them.

Kallie's heart was in her mouth. Was it the village kids, back to settle a score from the night before? Kallie knew Emilia thought they'd been just joking around but Kallie couldn't forget those blank eyes, those hypnotic movements – there was something weird about those kids.

Kallie spotted a faded umbrella on a shelf and moved towards it. If it came to a fight, she wouldn't be empty-handed.

'Who's there?' came Emilia's wobbling voice.

The footsteps paused. Then they quickened – *thump-thump* – and with a tumble, a figure fell down the last three steps and crashed into the nearest clothes rack. Emilia's torch revealed Ivan, dazed and confused, in a pile of petticoats.

'I thought you'd gone off to rehearse without me,'

he said, squinting up at them. 'Everyone's meeting in the theatre.'

'Sorry, mate,' said Emilia, helping Ivan to his feet. 'We lost track of time.'

'What is this place?' Ivan reached out a hand towards the nearest outfit but Emilia flapped it away.

'Nothing to see here,' said Emilia briskly. 'If my mum finds out we were here we'll be toast – so don't tell anyone.'

'Er . . . OK, but how did—'

'Less said the better. Honestly, Mum will skin us like bad bananas if she catches us!' Emilia shooed Ivan up the stairs. 'Coming, Kal?'

Kallie was still kneeling by the clothes rack. She watched Emilia follow Ivan up into the light, her heartbeat slowly returning to normal. She looked down at the parchment still clutched in her hand and, carefully as she could, she unfolded it. It was four sheets of curvy handwriting in a dark greenish ink. It was a letter. Her eye was drawn at once to the top of the page. One line jumped out and set her nerves jangling:

they came for her on the night of the Hay Moon: Ellsabet the Witch.

Chapter Thirteen

The letter was stowed in Kallie's back pocket as she, Emilia and Ivan hurried back to the theatre.

Kallie was bursting to read more. Did the writer of that letter know Ellsabet? Kallie felt that the more she discovered about Ellsabet, the more it would help her understand the curious goings-on of the last two days.

Unsurprisingly, since they hadn't had time to rehearse, Kallie, Emilia and Ivan's performance of the opening speech fell a bit flat. Emilia read out the lines and Kallie and Ivan made 'dramatic background noises', which sounded more like they were chewing food with their mouths open. Jackie pursed her lips disapprovingly but made no comment.

'The play!' announced Jackie, chivvying them back to their seats and holding up a stack of photocopied scripts. 'You will find your part on the top of your script. Besides the Storyteller, the Southern Lord, his son and the villainous North King, we have the Lord's

Household, the King's Courtiers, and the Narrators. Some of you may have more lines than others, but rest assured that you are all equally important and the production will not work unless each and every one of you plays your part to the best of your ability. We will read the first act before morning break.'

Kallie took her script and saw the name at the top: *Kallie Tamm – Astrologer (the King's Courtiers).*

Everyone was comparing parts. Most of the cast were smiling but there were a few disappointed frowns. It was no surprise that Marlow and Emilia were cast in the top roles; Marlow was the North King (his face glowing with glee as he took his script) and Emilia was the Storyteller.

'Nice one.' Kallie grinned. Emilia smiled back, pink-cheeked and pleased.

Kallie was happy with her role. She'd never want to be a main character; she had more fun making up her own characters on the side. Plus it meant fewer lines to stumble over. Although being one of the King's Courtiers meant a lot of scenes with Marlow.

She flicked quickly through the first act, her stomach fluttering uncomfortably at the prospect of reading aloud. She had a few lines in the second scene. Already some of the words looked tricky. She glanced sideways at Emilia, wondering if she had the guts to ask her friend for help – what if the words she couldn't read were actually really easy? Before she'd made up her mind, Violet called for silence and the read-through began.

Apart from the surging tension that filled her every time one of her lines approached, Kallie actually enjoyed it. The Astrologer had a couple of funny lines, like 'Great Orion's Belt! I see doom approaching on the horizon!' Kallie decided to do a pompous voice – rather like Mr Mildew's – which caused a few chuckles from the group. This also meant she could disguise the difficult words and pretend it was all part of her character's accent.

The gossip about her speech yesterday had died down, and although the rest of the cast weren't exactly overly friendly towards her, they weren't ignoring her any more. She suspected that having Emilia by her side had something to do with it.

When they finally left for break, Kallie caught Emilia's arm.

'I took something from the costume chamber,' whispered Kallie, 'and I think it's important.'

There wasn't a safe moment to read the letter until much later. After break, the cast returned to the read-through. *The King's Downfall* was an entertaining story with funny moments and dramatic sword fights between the Southern Lord and the King's Courtiers, passionate speeches from the Storyteller and even some stage magic from the North King, who experimented with dark enchantments to try and gain more power. But, of course, the heroes won out in the end – although, Kallie thought, the play seemed to end quite abruptly with the King falling off his horse on the battlefield.

Kallie was looking forward to rehearsing the sword fighting. She'd actually got quite interested in stage combat earlier that year and had learnt some fencing moves from videos online – which had ended with her accidentally jabbing a broom through the kitchen window.

During lunch, Dotty, the costumer, called people away to try on costumes so she could start adjusting them to fit. Kallie was presented with a billowing velvet cape covered with suns, moons and stars. Marlow, as the King, had the most splendid costume out of everyone: a flowing golden robe, decorated with gems that looked like real rubies.

'I heard Violet saying they're planning on using real pyrotechnics,' said Marlow, wafting his golden robe importantly. 'You know, for the battle scene and the King's magic tricks.'

'Pyro-what?' Ivan asked.

He was eyeing Marlow's costume with a longing expression; as one of the King's servants, Ivan's costume was basically a grey bedsheet with a hole for his head.

'Pyrotechnics,' sighed Marlow. 'Explosions, bangs and kapows!'

To illustrate his point, Marlow spun on his heel, stumbled on his overly long robe and knocked into Dotty, her arms full of neck ruffs.

'That's quite enough banging and kapowing,' snapped Dotty, chasing Marlow back to the changing room.

Kallie caught Emilia's eye from across the room and they both snorted behind their scripts.

After lunch, the cast were called back to the theatre to finish reading Act Two. So it wasn't until after a dinner of cheesy pasta (with extra cheese) that Kallie and Emilia finally had time to escape. They hurried down to the empty campsite, their pockets stuffed with Burn's homemade brownies. Smudge scampered behind them.

The sun had dropped, orange and wan, but the birds were still chatting noisily in the hedgerows.

They squeezed into Kallie's tent and sat on the mattress, their feet sticking out of the open entrance. Kallie's stomach somersaulted as they laid the letter between them.

'Shall I read it aloud?' offered Emilia. 'Things are always more dramatic when they're read out loud.'

Kallie nodded, too excited to speak. Emilia read in a low voice:

Merricombe, 1600

Dear-heart,

I write to share my story and the story of one I have lost. I shall lay down the events that led to that fateful night when they came for her on the night of the Hay Moon: Ellsabet the Witch.

First, I must go further back, to the day she arrived in Merricombe. It was a breezy summer's morning when word reached us of a stranger on Father's land. Father suspected thieves – hungering after our mutton – and sent my brother John to challenge them. Only a bold trickster would dare trespass on the Graveheart estate. I was told to stay in the house but I, Rose Graveheart, was thirteen and ready for an adventure. So I followed secretly behind John.

She was sitting by the stream, hair black as night and eyes sharp as a fox. Her white face was flushed and her dress splattered with mud. John stumbled to a stop and I could tell he thought she was beautiful. She held a scroll of parchment, a quill and a pot of ink on her knee. Her hand raced across the page – I had never seen anyone write like that. Least of all a girl of sixteen who dressed like a peasant! John had taught me my letters but I was still slow. Writing was for wealthy landlords and men of the church.

When John had regained his senses, he hailed her and brought her back up to the house. Father gave her food and comforts and once we were gathering about the fire, the girl gave her name: Ellsabet. She was a playwright, a storyteller. She told us that a terrible disaster had befallen her village. But she had escaped, climbed mountains and forded rivers, travelling for many days before reaching our lands. She would not tell us what the disaster had been and Father did not press her. Once her tale was done, he bade her stay as long as she needed. I knew John would be happy about that. From the silly way he looked, I knew he was already half in love with Ellsabet.

Before the winter frosts had arrived, Ellsabet and John were married. They took a little home on the edge of the village, called Moss Cottage. I visited Ellsabet most days, while John worked on Father's land. Soon we had become as close as two sisters. She helped me with my letters and I helped her bake bread. She never talked about her past but I knew it still troubled her. She still kept many secrets. Sometimes she would journey out of Merricombe and return with pamphlets that she would study for days. Several times peculiar people came to the village to speak with her – elderly poets and scholars.

When the days turned warmer, the village children came to the garden and Ellsabet would write little plays for them – which she and I would act together. I baked them biscuits made with currants and oats, but it was the plays that fed them most. Stories of battles and heroes. I loved Ellsabet's stories. They made me feel braver. They made me imagine all the adventures I could go on, and I began to dream that I could do more with my little life in Merricombe.

She was writing a play for John's friends to perform. A play about a Storyteller. Some had grumbled about a woman playwright but John had stood by her. He said if our Good Queen Bess could govern our country, then his wife could be a playwright. John was building her a theatre in the woods, using stone from an old cow shed. Ellsabet told me how she'd once journeyed to London and seen a theatre as big as a cathedral. 'A theatre is the most magical place,' she told me, 'a place where people share stories and dream as one.'

I should have known those happy days would never last.

It was summer when the rumours started. Almost a year after she had arrived. The summer sun was high, the days long and dry. It began with a whisper, a bad word and a suspicious look, and then the stories turned cruel and bitter. The Innkeeper called for Ellsabet's play to be stopped. Even John's friends agreed.

They said that Ellsabet had tricked John into marrying her. That she was poisoning the village children with her stories – filling their heads with nonsense, turning them into daydreamers. That she had dried up the stream with a spell. That she was a witch.

Father forbade me from seeing Ellsabet and John. He spoke so strangely; it was as if he had forgotten John was his son. For the first time in my life, I argued back. Like a hero in one of Ellsabet's stories! Father stared back at me, his eyes full of fog, like a sleepwalker who had escaped his bed. He was not *himself – it was as if he had been enchanted. So I took my parchment and my best quills, and I ran away, down to Moss Cottage. When I told them, Ellsabet's face went white and her hands trembled.*

She looked at John and said: 'He is here.'

Her words set me shivering.

'Who?' I asked. 'Who is here?'

'I have seen these signs before, Rose. Merricombe is in danger and I fear it is because of me.'

The one who had turned her village against her. The one who had taken her family. The one she had run from. He had found her. She had always known he would.

Ellsabet was no witch. There are some things more terrible than witches out there.

He will be strongest at the Hay Moon, she told me, for he—

Emilia stopped reading, her voice fading away. Kallie looked over at her. There was no more letter. Emilia's usually rosy face was pale in the low sunset. Smudge was curled in the open entrance to the tent, like a furry mat, his green eyes fixed on Rose Graveheart's letter.

'Where's the rest of it?' said Kallie. There was a strange ringing in her ears, as if Rose's words were still exploding inside her head. 'We should go back to the costume chamber.'

'It's too late. Mum will be annoyed if I'm out late.' Emilia winced, glancing towards Hollowstar House; people were starting to stroll back to the campsite, a few using their torches as the evening drew in. 'We wouldn't have enough time. Kallie, do you think this letter is, like, for real?'

'Yes,' said Kallie firmly. 'I trust Rose.'

She'd never felt so certain of anything before.

'But the story of Ellsabet the Witch is part of Merricombe history,' said Emilia, shaking her head. 'What about all the Ellsabet the Witch stuff they sell in the village?'

'Just because a story has been told a lot, it doesn't mean it's true,' said Kallie, frowning. 'Think about it, it's so one-sided: the villagers clearly didn't like Ellsabet and it's their version of the story that has survived.'

'You're blowing my mind,' said Emilia, sinking back on her elbows.

'The villagers must have been suspicious of her from the start,' said Kallie grimly. 'She was different – she'd always been an outsider to them.'

Kallie's face grew hot as she imagined how Ellsabet must have felt – vilified by the place that she thought had become her new home. Even Rose's father had changed his mind after he'd heard the rumours. She could see Ellsabet in her head: a young and wilful woman, no longer the witch steeped in suspicion. Ellsabet was more than a scowling witchy face on a grubby tea towel! Kallie felt a rush of solidarity for her.

'Do you think it was our play?' said Emilia. 'The one Ellsabet was writing?'

'Yeah – it must be.' Kallie nodded. 'It says she wrote it for John's friends to perform.'

'And who is this man following Ellsabet?' pondered Emilia.

'He's the reason Ellsabet had to run away,' said Kallie, her throat dry. 'He must have had something to do with the disaster at her village. He seems powerful.'

'Powerful?' Emilia stared at her. 'What, like – he's a witch or a magician? Or something like that?'

They both looked down at the final page.

There are some things more terrible than witches out there.

'Is a magician worse than a witch?' said Emilia doubtfully. 'Or maybe he was just a really mean guy?'

'Rose's father . . .' Kallie was choosing her words

98

carefully. 'Rose says it was like he'd been enchanted . . . "eyes full of fog", she wrote. And she said it was like he couldn't remember his son.'

She paused. There was something spookily familiar in Rose's description.

'"Enchanted" is a bit strong, isn't it?' said Emilia, pulling a dubious face. 'Maybe Rose's father was just scared by all the gossip.'

Kallie bit her tongue. Rose's father sounded a lot like Arley and his friends, with their blank-eyed stares. But Emilia would probably find the idea far-fetched.

'And what's a Hay Moon?' said Emilia, squinting at the letter.

'No idea.' Kallie shrugged. 'Maybe it's a saying like "once in a blue moon"?'

The shadows were beginning to yawn across the meadow now and Wildstormers were returning to their tents. Kallie carefully collected the pages of the letter and zipped them safely inside her rucksack.

Much later, when Emilia had gone back to Hollowstar House, thoughts were still chasing themselves around Kallie's head as she lay in her sleeping bag. The letter was worrying her. Emilia didn't seem to understand. She was interested in the story of Ellsabet, but that was all it was to Emilia: a story. To Kallie, it felt like a warning.

Ellsabet's play had returned, the theatre had been reopened after four hundred years and now the villagers were grumbling again. The Historical Society and Mr Mildew were threatening the Wildstorm production, just like the villagers had complained against Ellsabet's play in her time. And just like Rose's father, Arley had stared at his old friend Emilia with foggy eyes as if he didn't even recognise her.

Kallie rolled over and stared at the grey canvas wall.

There was another player in this mystery – the unknown 'him'. It was after Ellsabet heard about Rose's father that she knew 'he' had found her. He had turned the village against her. Did he really have the power to – it seemed outlandish to even consider – *enchant* people? Kallie thought back to her childhood books of fairy tales: dark magic that made people act strangely or perform tasks with no memory of doing them.

Kallie shivered. She had to know what was in the second half of Rose's letter. She had to know more.

Something bad had come to Merricombe all those years ago. And if the events of the past were repeating themselves, surely that could mean only one thing. The one who had hunted Ellsabet had returned to Merricombe once more.

Chapter Fourteen

Midnight and the garden of Hollowstar House was dappled in grey starlight. There was no one awake to hear the footsteps, treading through the wet grass.

He was stronger now. Thanks to a little help, he was more than a shadow.

The cool air stung his skin but his teeth were bared in a grin. It was glorious to be back. Just like old times. Back to his old tricks! Visiting old haunts. He was getting quite nostalgic . . .

Time had made some unexpected changes in the village. Horseless carriages with four wheels, flat mirrors showing moving pictures and little nut-shaped objects people kept putting in their ears! It was all most peculiar.

But the people smelt the same. They had the same fears. The same weaknesses.

Outside Hollowstar House, he moved softly, his eyes picking up every movement of the wind and every twitch in the undergrowth. Something quivered in the window of the house – a black cat, staring out at him. He hissed at it and the cat backed out of sight, fur standing on end. He smiled.

Slipping through shadow, he wound his way through the trees and approached the theatre. What an ugly place it was. It made his skin crawl and his hands shake, anger tightening like a spring in his chest. Even now, four hundred years later, his insides burnt as he thought of that troublemaker. Ellsabet Graveheart. Those defiant eyes and quick-witted words. What a pest she had been! The first one to ever escape him. The first one to . . . well, that was all in the past. He would have his revenge . . . one way or another.

And now there was the girl. She would be taken care of – so would her friend. After the Hay Moon, they would be easy to manage.

He pressed a hand to the theatre door. Locked. As he knew it would be. He crept around its walls. Beside him, he could feel the theatre creaking uneasily as if it knew he was there. The theatre could not keep him out any more. He raised a hand in the air and figures emerged from the darkness, walking in unison as if to the beat of a silent drum. Tonight he would have some fun.

CHAPTER FIFTEEN

The next morning, Kallie knew that something had happened.

There was a nervous energy in the campsite. People darted from group to group, sharing secrets like the sparrows in the hedges. The air was heavy with heat; low clouds furrowed the sky.

It was Wednesday, three days until the show, and the cast were due to do their first full rehearsal of Act One that morning. But this wasn't performance excitement, this was something else.

Kallie met Emilia in the garden.

'Quick! It's the theatre,' said Emilia. 'Mum and Violet saw it this morning.'

'Saw what?'

Kallie hurried after Emilia, her mind racing wildly. Jackie, Violet and Ray were standing in the doorway to the theatre. Kallie's heart leapt into her mouth as she saw what lay inside. The canvas backdrop had been slashed; the starlit country scene Ray had painted was torn in two. Chairs had been smashed and broken. The rack of costumes Dotty had been working on was almost empty, capes and petticoats pillaged or else thrown on to the floor.

'I thought the theatre was locked,' whispered Kallie. 'They would have needed the key.'

The same key that Arley had been looking for two nights ago on Fallow Hill.

'I think . . .' Emilia's eyes darted nervously. 'I think maybe they used a different entrance . . .'

Without a word, they fled around the outside. Kallie stumbled to a stop, her nerves twisting. The secret door to the chamber was flung wide open. The brambles and nettles that had guarded the entrance had been trampled into the mud. Trails of muddy footprints battered the stone steps, down into the darkness.

'There must be a way into the main theatre through here,' Emilia moaned and she headed for the steps.

Kallie followed her, more slowly, half scared of what they'd find below.

They both had their Wildstorm pocket torches and their beams flashed around the chamber. Half the costumes had vanished and those remaining were dangling off their hangers. The broken jewellery was scattered over the shelves and hats had been plucked of feathers. The pain in Kallie's chest was horrible. Who knew how long these costumes had hung here in peace before now? How could they have been so stupid as to leave the secret door open?

Kallie swung her torch, no longer scared of the mannequins in the corners, desperate to find the rest of Rose Graveheart's letter – but there was nothing.

'Emilia! Kallie!'

Kallie jumped – a bulb sprang on above them. Jackie was standing on the stairs, her hand on a light switch they'd failed to find in the dark.

'Ivan was right, you two have been exploring when you should have been rehearsing!' Jackie's face was cold with fury.

Beside Kallie, Emilia looked green with guilt. Jackie might be Emilia's mum, but Kallie knew they wouldn't be getting any special treatment.

'I cannot believe you would treat this theatre with such little respect,' snarled Jackie, 'poking around and unlocking doors that, I don't suppose you ever considered, were locked for a reason! This chamber has been safely guarded for hundreds of years before you two came along.'

'You knew?' Emilia seemed unable to hold herself

back. 'And you didn't tell me?'

'This is my theatre, Emilia, and it is my right to keep certain parts of it hidden. There is a time and a place for secrets to be revealed.'

Jackie brushed through the chamber and swept aside a grey curtain to uncover a small hole in the wall. Beyond, Kallie could see underneath the stage. One of the trapdoors in the stage floor was open, and they could see up into the theatre itself. Jackie's gaze snapped back to them.

'And now because of your exploring, costumes have been stolen or ruined, and props have been taken.'

Kallie felt a gut punch of guilt.

'We're sorry! Honestly! We didn't mean for anything to happen,' Emilia pleaded.

Kallie nodded in agreement.

'Your punishment will be to clean up the mess you have caused.' Jackie scowled. 'First, eat your breakfast – you're no use to anyone with empty stomachs. Go to the kitchen and I want you back here in ten minutes.'

They left without protest, hurrying up the stone steps into the light, Kallie's stomach curling as she thought how the other cast members would react when they found out what had happened.

Kallie had never seen Emilia look so dejected as they

took their cheese and mushroom omelettes from Burn. The old cook seemed colder than usual and Kallie wondered if he'd already heard about their misdeeds. The countdown – *3 DAYS TO GO* – wafted in the wind and Kallie felt another wave of guilt. The maimed set and costumes would mean hours more work for the Wildstorm staff, time they didn't have.

'It's all my fault,' muttered Emilia, as they sat down. 'I should have thought to check the door was closed.'

'I was the one who wanted to explore,' said Kallie. 'It was a mistake.'

'I bet it was Arley and his new friends.' Emilia sniffed. 'He must hate Wildstorm now! How could they do this?'

'Unless they weren't fully themselves,' muttered Kallie darkly.

But Emilia didn't seem to be listening. She was staring down at her plate, as if she was considering face-planting in her omelette.

'I hate this,' Emilia mumbled. 'How are we going to do the play without half the costumes? It's not just those old costumes that have gone – it's ours too. Mum's worked so hard on Wildstorm. She does everything – you know she spends days finding schools that don't have a drama club so she can send them flyers. I don't want anyone to stop Wildstorm!'

'We won't let them,' said Kallie firmly; she hated seeing Emilia like this. 'This isn't going to stop the play. Your mum couldn't be stopped by *an army* of Mr Mildews.'

'Guess not.' Emilia shrugged, but she gave a half-grin as she started on her breakfast.

Kallie could see how much Wildstorm meant to Emilia – and Jackie. She realised if it hadn't been for Jackie, Kallie would never have seen that flyer in her school library and never would have come to Wildstorm. Kallie liked how theatre was a bond through their family. Her own mum was supportive but didn't really care about theatre the way Kallie did. She wondered how the Masters family had come to own the Merricombe theatre.

Kallie didn't mention her theories about what might be causing Arley and the boys to act in such an uncharacteristic way. Emilia was determined to find other excuses for their behaviour. But Emilia hadn't heard those boys chanting in the woods, Kallie reminded herself. That mystery was still bothering her.

Armed with brooms and dustpans, Kallie and Emilia started tidying the destruction in the theatre. Violet was sympathetic and helped them stack chairs and gather the remaining costumes into a pile. They were still working when the rest of the cast arrived after breakfast, their stares burning into the back of Kallie's head. She wished she could take the mop and wipe off Marlow's smug grin.

'Quiet please. Take a seat, Marlow,' Jackie boomed. 'As you can see, a handful of no-gooders broke into the theatre last night. The set will need to be repainted and the costumes will have to be patched up. But we will not let them stop us. I know we are stronger than that. If anyone knows anything about who may have done this, speak to me or Violet. Now, I want the Narrators in that corner and everyone in scene one onstage. The play must go on.'

Despite Jackie's rousing speech, the morning rehearsal was subdued and energy was low. Even though Jackie hadn't said it, everyone seemed to know Kallie and Emilia had something to do with the break-in. Kallie knew how Ellsabet must have felt with the whole village against her, unable to defend herself. Kallie felt worse for Emilia: she had her eyes down and her neck had almost disappeared into her hoodie.

Kallie somehow managed to get through the morning, by ignoring the stares and repeating her lines over and over in her head. The others in her group giggled as she stumbled over her words, accidentally saying 'plants' instead of 'planets' so it sounded like she was warning the King about a giant garden in the sky. Violet, who was directing their scene, quickly silenced the gigglers.

'Come on, guys, we all make mistakes,' said Violet cheerfully. 'Let's move on.'

Kallie could sense Violet keeping an eye on her throughout the rehearsal and although she knew she meant to be kind, it made Kallie feel like even more of a loser.

After lunch, the cast were given the afternoon off to go into the village – this was a Wildstorm mid-week tradition and Kallie had been looking forward to it. The village was the backdrop to Ellsabet's story and Kallie was keen to see it for herself. But in the rush to the door, Jackie called Kallie and Emilia back.

'There is more work to do before you go,' said Jackie. 'You can help Dotty with the costumes. What's left of them.'

Kallie and Emilia exchanged grudging looks. But it wasn't so bad. Dotty was working on her sewing machine in a corner and didn't pay them much attention as they put the remaining costumes in piles to be repaired.

'I see the thieves didn't want your costume,' said Emilia, holding up the spangled velvet cape of the Astrologer. 'Can't blame them.'

'Hey! I like it!' Kallie laughed, pulling it away from her.

'It's like a giant furry duvet,' teased Emilia good-naturedly; her spirits never seemed low for long.

Kallie was running her hand over the little embroidered suns and moons decorating the cape. She gave a cry of surprise.

'The Hay Moon! Em, it's here!'

There, sewn around the hem of Kallie's costume, were a series of coloured moons, each with a tiny name embroidered above it – *Flower Moon*, *Strawberry Moon* and *Hay Moon* – with a month below each of them.

'It's a different moon for each month,' said Kallie excitedly. 'Strawberry Moon for June. Hay Moon is July.'

'So it's the Hay Moon now?'

'Just like in Rose's letter,' muttered Kallie. 'They took Ellsabet on the Hay Moon.'

Here was another hint that the past was repeating itself – just like a play with new actors reading an old script.

'We need to find the second half of the letter,' said Kallie firmly.

'Come on, then,' said Emilia, with a quick glance in

Dotty's direction. 'Let's go and check the chamber again now.'

Dotty was absorbed in her sewing machine so she didn't notice them creep away and clamber under the stage and through the grey curtain, back into the costume chamber. They searched quickly; it was a lot easier with the light on. They checked every inch of the remaining costumes for more parchment hidden in the fabric, but there was no sign of Rose's letter or any other letters. They hurried back to the auditorium.

'So if it's not in the costume chamber, it was either stolen with the costumes or it was never there to begin with,' said Emilia.

'If only there was some place where we could look up old letters written hundreds of years ago,' sighed Kallie, sitting down on the broken chair.

'But, Kallie, there is!' Emilia laughed. 'The Historical Society! They have an office in the village. Even if we don't find the second half of the letter, they're bound to have something useful on Ellsabet or Rose!'

'Brilliant!' Kallie grinned. 'But are we allowed inside?'

'Nope,' said Emilia, her eyes bright. 'We'll have to break in.'

Chapter Sixteen

Jackie let Kallie and Emilia go after she was satisfied they'd done enough cleaning up. Only half of the costumes and props remained – hardly enough for a full production – and Kallie felt a swoop of guilt as she saw sadness in Jackie's eyes.

Kallie and Emilia walked out towards the village, formulating their plan for how to break into the Historical Society office. The day had turned bright again, the blue sky laced with thin clouds. The road felt hot underfoot, and the hedgerows bobbed with wild flowers and darting butterflies.

It was a ten-minute walk to the village. Every so often the hedges gave way to squat cottages with thatched roofs, roses crawling up their walls. Kallie wondered if one of the cottages had been Moss Cottage, Ellsabet and John Graveheart's home, if it was still standing.

They turned a corner and came out on the edge of

a market square. The village shops were decorated with hanging baskets of pink geraniums. A church, snug and sleepy, nestled to the side of the square. A few Wildstormers were sitting on the bank of a stream, finishing off ice creams; Kallie spotted Ivan licking a chocolate cone almost as big as his head.

Kallie imagined Rose and Ellsabet strolling towards this very same market square, baskets in the crooks of their arms ready to be filled with fresh apples, bread and cheese.

'It's all a bit peculiar, isn't it?' said Emilia, as they walked on. 'The Hay Moon stuff and the villagers suddenly hating Wildstorm. It's kind of like it's all happening again. Is that silly?'

'No, that's what I was thinking,' said Kallie keenly.

'This is it.' Emilia pointed. 'The Historical Society has an office round the back of the church.'

The churchyard was overgrown with yellow flowers, the gravestones cracked and crumbling.

'Which way do we go?' asked Kallie, but Emilia had stopped in her tracks, the flush draining from her face.

Kallie stared from Emilia's panicked eyes to the churchyard, confused – but then she saw them. The three village boys standing in a far corner. They weren't speaking. They weren't doing anything. Just standing there, like puppets without strings, their eyes full of fog.

'We should come back later,' said Kallie, her heart thumping, but Emilia didn't respond. 'Come on, Em.'

Emilia was pale and clammy. Kallie took her arm and backed away from the church wall. The boys gave no sign that they knew they were being watched; they simply stood there staring, staring. Kallie steered Emilia across the road to the Marmalade Café.

Once she'd got her inside, Kallie hastily ordered two lemonades and a slice of Victoria sponge with extra clotted cream. After gulping down her lemonade and several spoonfuls of cream (leaving the cake for Kallie), Emilia looked a little better.

'Sorry,' Emilia sighed. 'That was just a bit . . . freaky. Seeing them all standing there. And Arley – if you knew him, you'd know he wouldn't do anything like that. Even for a joke. I don't understand, Kallie, what's going on?'

Kallie hesitated. She knew it was time to share her suspicions with Emilia, however far-fetched they seemed.

'I think it's just like Rose wrote in her letter,' Kallie began. 'The same thing happened to her father; he couldn't even remember John was his son. I think the same thing has happened to Arley. Rose thought her father had been . . . enchanted. It's got something to do with the man who followed Ellsabet to Merricombe. And now it's happening again, I think he . . . he might be back.'

Emilia was gazing at her with her mouth half-open.

'But it's just a theory,' said Kallie quickly. 'I know it's weird – but you saw those boys. They're not acting normally.'

'No, they're not,' Emilia agreed. 'I think I need my own cake for this.'

A second slice of Victoria sponge was quickly ordered. Kallie recognised the man who served them as Mr Dixson, who'd delivered the biscuits to Wildstorm on her first day. Yet his cheery manner was gone. He banged the plate on to the table and stalked away, muttering about 'theatre ruffians'. Clearly the ill-feeling towards the Wildstormers was spreading fast, even poisoning those who used to support them.

'So Arley has become enchanted?' said Emilia, digging into the cake. 'Is that why they had those tattoos on their arms? What does C stand for?'

'It could be the name of the person who did this to them,' said Kallie excitably. 'C for, um . . .'

'Cake? I mean – Colin?' suggested Emilia. 'But the man who followed Ellsabet – this magician man or

116

whoever – he was around four hundred years ago. Surely it can't be the same guy?'

'If he can enchant people, maybe staying alive for four hundred years is easy,' said Kallie darkly. 'I've just had a strange feeling these last few days, like there's something bad around. Like the night of the Wildstorm Challenge, I thought maybe someone was watching us in the woods.'

'You think this guy is hiding in the woods?'

Kallie nodded, but she still wasn't entirely sure.

'But why now? Why – wait a minute!' Emilia dropped her fork with excitement. 'It's the play, isn't it? It's set something off. Like when people steal things from ancient Egyptian tombs? They awake some sleeping evil thing!'

The colour was back in Emilia's cheeks and Kallie suddenly felt a swoop of excited determination. She had been sorry to see Emilia so shaken up but now she had her on side, they could fix this mystery together. Find out what evil was lurking in Merricombe and save Arley and his friends before things got worse.

'Your mum could have found the script in the costume chamber,' said Kallie thoughtfully.

'Yeah, I still can't believe she didn't tell me about the chamber,' grumbled Emilia. 'OK. Let's say finding the play releases this person and he's back in Merricombe, creeping around, making people enchanted. What does he want?'

'I don't know,' said Kallie. 'Maybe the theatre *is* cursed and this is what happens whenever someone tries to use it. But Ellsabet wanted the theatre built and we know she wasn't actually a witch.'

They both sat in silence for a few minutes, eating their cakes and thinking.

Looking around the Marmalade Café, Kallie saw that Emilia hadn't been kidding about the village being obsessed with Ellsabet the Witch. There was a whole wall dedicated to paintings of her. They were all similar to the image on the tea towel Marlow had brought to the Wildstorm Challenge: a bony, scowling figure dressed all in black. None of them looked like the Ellsabet in Kallie's mind. Kallie's gaze was drawn to one painting of a messy-haired Ellsabet holding a broomstick and standing in front of a green cottage. As far as Kallie could tell, they'd got Ellsabet all wrong.

'And there's another thing,' said Emilia. 'Didn't Rose's letter say something about him being stronger at the Hay Moon? Well, it's a full moon in three days – the night of the play. If it's really him then we don't have much time.'

'Rose survived him once, or she wouldn't have been able to write that letter,' said Kallie. 'She must have information that can help us. We need the rest of the letter. Right now, our best bet is the Historical Society.'

'Arley won't be stuck like that for ever, will he?' said Emilia, in an uncharacteristically small voice.

'No,' said Kallie, 'we won't let him.'

Kallie scrunched up her napkin, staring out of the window towards the churchyard. Her mind was full of black-cloaked magicians with red eyes, clicking their fingers as an army of Enchanted souls marched in unison. Despite her determined words, Kallie was nervous. She'd dealt with monsters and villains in her own plays, but this wasn't a story she was writing. This mystery was very real.

Chapter Seventeen

The Historical Society office was a small room at the back of the church. Two society members could fit comfortably side by side to sort through old diaries and dusty paintings sent in by hopeful history buffs. The society's job was to separate the factual from the fake. A certificate of approval from the society was a mark of authenticity – which often added a hundred or so pounds to the price of the object. More than once, a twee old lady had tried to sneak in an 'eighteenth-century watercolour' that was actually their grandson's finger painting. Everything was checked and double-checked. Mr Mildew ran a tight ship.

The key to the office was kept on the vicar's keychain, along with several other keys that the vicar had long ago forgotten what they unlocked. The vicar was, that afternoon, watering the bulbs he had planted that spring and humming a pop song to himself.

Kallie and Emilia, hidden behind a hedge, watched

the vicar whistling and wiggling along the flowerbeds in the churchyard.

'If we keep down, we can get to the back of the church without him seeing us,' said Emilia. 'There's a window into the office. Then you climb through, and I'll keep watch.'

'I don't mind keeping watch,' whispered Kallie, a little nervously.

'I'll give you a leg-up,' said Emilia reassuringly. 'I'm more of a local than you so if the vicar sees me hanging around, I can always talk about my mum to distract him – the vicar likes her.'

The two of them started to crawl behind the hedge, dry leaves and twigs collecting in Kallie's long hair. When they'd reached the back of the church, Emilia made a small opening under the hedge with her foot. The vicar was out of sight and the window to the Historical Society was only a few steps away. Emilia was about to dive through the hole but Kallie grabbed her arm.

'No! Look!' she whispered.

The village boys – the Enchanted, as Kallie had come to think of them – had appeared at the other end of the churchyard. Kallie held her breath, her heart beating wildly. There was no doubt about it: something evil resonated from these children, like ripples in a black lake.

Emilia had her hand over her mouth, worried she might cry out. Every muscle in Kallie's body tensed as the Enchanted came closer and closer. But they passed their hiding place without a glance and Kallie relaxed. The boys disappeared around the corner of the church.

'We'll have to be quick,' said Kallie.

The two of them squeezed under the hedge and hurried up to the window. Emilia knelt down so Kallie could put her foot on her friend's knee and hoisted herself up to the window frame. The pane was stiff but after a tremendous push, it sprang open.

'Go, go, go!' hissed Emilia, pushing Kallie up over the sill.

Kallie came through the window a little faster than she would have liked, and hit the stone floor with a *thwack!* She stood up, rubbing her arms, and looked around.

She saw rows and rows of shelves, stuffed with hundreds of dusty folders. In the only space that wasn't filled up with shelving hung a cracked yellow map of Merricombe village. On a desk in the centre were more folders and papers, sorted into neat wire baskets. Each inch of the room was organised in a way only those in the Historical Society could possibly understand.

Kallie took a calming breath. Somewhere in this room

might be answers – possibly even the second half of Rose's letter. But the only problem was Kallie had no idea where to start. She and Emilia had agreed she had ten minutes to search. Any longer was too risky.

She started taking folders off the shelves and peeking inside. There were lots of old letters here but nothing written in green ink. Kallie stepped up to the desk and opened one of the notebooks. It was a log of artefacts that had been taken out.

Mrs Scratch had taken out **Deaths & Births Docs 1500–1501** (D-14-F).

Mr Mildew had picked up **MS 1600** (F-25-F) and **Medieval fire tongs** (G-3-B).

What Mr Mildew was going to be using medieval fire tongs for, Kallie had no idea. Toasting historical marshmallows?

Next to the logbook was a handwritten list titled *STOLEN ITEMS*, and she remembered Mr Mildew saying to Jackie that there had been a break-in the day before. Kallie ran her fingers down the list, noting the curious titles.

Warding Off Evil by Fredrick Frank (1850)

Posies and Poisons: Good Luck Charms in 16th-Century Britain by S. McCaffrey (1975)

Bad Spirits in Ancient Europe by Professor A. Kosmatka (1992)

The thief who had stolen them must have had very specific interests. Kallie wondered if the books contained any information about enchantments and how to stop them. She dropped the list back on the table, panic beginning to rise inside her. She needed to find something!

She squeezed past the desk, heading for more shelves, but her elbow caught a stack of folders, sending them cascading to the floor. With a nervous glance at the door, she ducked to scoop them up but then froze. A label on the top folder read:

Ellsabet the Witch – Trial, 1600

Kallie sank down and opened the folder on her knees. Her hands shaking, she turned the pages. Everything was written in slanting handwriting that was difficult to decipher. Kallie took a deep breath; it was always harder to read when she was nervous, but she muttered the words aloud as she read, skipping anything she couldn't work out:

To the Honourable and Worship His Majesty's
Justices of Peace of the West Country. We whose
names are written below, being good residents
of the village of Merricombe for many peaceful
years, do claim as follows:

That she Ellsabet Graveheart be a witch and has
consorted in witchcraft and unnatural wrongs.
This hateful girl has brought diabolical evils to
our lives.

Ellsabet has been witnessed writing spells and
other evil words. And with these spells – which
she did call 'stories' – she has turned our children
into fools who question their superiors. She has
been walking by meadows in which after the
sheep turned thin and gravely died. Crops have
withered in the sun and the harvest has been
meagre since Ellsabet arrived. Our fair innkeeper
claims that she has met with many devilish
characters, strangers whom many believe to be
vagabonds. And when she coughs, up comes ink
and green feathers from her evil belly! Worst of
all, she has enchanted one John Graveheart, the
good son of wealthy landlord Graveheart, and
tricked this man into a false marriage and made

him build a stage where she planned to poison many with her evil tales.

We know her to be guilty of these crimes. Thus, in respect of the Witchcraft Act of 1563 passed by our fair Queen Elizabeth, her punishment is to be burnt on Fallow Hill this night. May we vanquish these bad spirits she has brought into our village.

So signed the village elders, good men of this parish.

Kallie checked to see if any of the names started with the letter C, but none of them did. Kallie remembered Rose recounting how Ellsabet met with elderly poets and scholars – could these people be the 'vagabonds' the villagers had seen her with? Why had Ellsabet met with them? Kallie's heart twisted thinking of how a whisper – a gossiping story – had resulted in the death of an innocent woman: a playwright. She'd never realised stories could be so dangerous.

There was a shuffling noise from the corridor and Kallie twisted around. She'd completely forgotten to check the door was locked. Quickly and quietly, she moved across the room, holding her breath, and stretched out a hand to turn the key – but the shuffling footsteps outside paused and to Kallie's horror there was a knock at the door.

'Is that you in there, Mr Mildew?' came the voice of the vicar.

Kallie's throat went dry.

'Mildew . . . ? Hello?' There was a squeak and the door handle turned.

Kallie steadied herself.

'I wish to be alone!' Kallie hissed, hoping she'd caught Mr Mildew's self-important voice.

There was a pause outside the door; Kallie wondered if the vicar had bought it. Impersonating Mr Mildew in a rehearsal was one thing, but would it work on someone who actually knew him?

'Um . . . very good,' mumbled the vicar's voice. 'I'll be outside when you've finished. Just pruning my petunias.'

The footsteps faded away and Kallie leant against the door.

'That was excellent!'

She jumped and turned to see Emilia's eyes and nose peering over the windowsill.

'You found anything?' Emilia whispered. 'I can hear the boys marching around again – we'd better go before they catch us.'

Kallie hastily picked up the folder with Ellsabet's trial notes and placed it back on the desk. She glanced once more at the shelves; if Rose's letter was here, there was no time to find it now. She hurried to the window but before she reached it, the old map on the wall caught her eye. It was a beautiful, hand-drawn plan of Merricombe, inky roads weaving through smudged meadows. There was no date but it looked extremely old; there were fewer houses and no theatre, but the market square and church were in the same place. As Kallie's eyes travelled down the map, she saw the label *Moss Cottage*. The home of Ellsabet and John Graveheart. She stepped closer. The cottage was on a corner where the road bent in a sharp U-turn, just at the foot of Fallow Hill. And with a thrill, Kallie realised that Moss Cottage was in exactly the same spot as Hollowstar House was today.

Chapter Eighteen

There was no sign of the Enchanted as Kallie and Emilia hurried around the side of the church, trying to look as if they were enjoying an innocent afternoon stroll and hadn't just been poking around forbidden historical documents.

Kallie couldn't believe she hadn't realised it before. It was so obvious.

'So Ellsabet and John lived in our house!' exclaimed Emilia, when Kallie had told her. 'Hollowstar House used to be called Moss Cottage?'

'Exactly.' Kallie grinned. 'I wonder who lived in the cottage after Ellsabet and John.' She was thinking about how many families had passed through it before it reached Jackie and Emilia. 'Your mum doesn't like talking about Ellsabet, does she? Do you know why?'

'She hates the way the villagers always go on about Ellsabet the Witch,' sighed Emilia. 'Says it's made-up nonsense to make money. She's got a point – the bakery even sells Ellsabet-shaped cream buns.'

Kallie thought back to the picture hanging in the Marmalade Café of Ellsabet standing in front of a green cottage. Surely Jackie knew the history of Hollowstar House, knew the connection to Ellsabet. She wondered what else the director knew about.

'How long has your family owned Hollowstar House?' asked Kallie, as they turned a corner of the church. 'You don't think—'

'It's them,' hissed Emilia and Kallie fell silent at once.

The real Mr Mildew was standing outside the church doors, leaning on his cane. Beside him stood the three village boys, all glassy-eyed and huddled together. Kallie was surprised Mr Mildew didn't notice anything strange about the boys but he wasn't looking at them as he said, 'Run along, boys. It's rude to loiter.'

The three of them walked out of the churchyard like silent soldiers. Kallie felt cold as she watched them go.

The vicar came hurrying down the steps.

'Oh, there you are! So sorry to have disturbed you earlier.'

Kallie saw Mr Mildew raise an eyebrow questioningly but he didn't comment; perhaps the vicar was always apologising about something.

'What is that, may I ask?' Mr Mildew pointed to the colourful sheet of paper in the vicar's hand.

'Poster for the Wildstorm Theatre Camp's show,' said the vicar cheerfully. 'I thought I'd pop it on the noticeboard.'

'Is that wise, Mermin?' Mr Mildew's voice was icy. 'The Wildstorm play is demonic drivel written by Ellsabet the Witch. Wildstorm is bringing disrepute to the village. Children can be so dangerous.'

The vicar looked down at the poster nervously, as if worried it might be dangerous too. Mr Mildew's eyes swivelled to fix on Kallie and Emilia. Emilia scowled back at him. A small group of elderly ladies had pottered up the path to the church and stopped to form an audience.

'That play will unleash evil if we don't stop it!' gabbled one of the ladies. 'Wildstorm is a stain on our countryside.'

'You can't trust actors, you know, Vicar.' Her friend nodded. 'They're always lying about something.'

'You see, Mermin?' Mr Mildew smiled widely. 'Those Wildstormers mean trouble.'

He tapped his cane on the flagstones as if underlining the word.

'That's not true!' snarled Emilia, glaring at Mr

Mildew. 'Mum's followed all your stupid rules, so why don't you just leave us alone?'

Kallie could see the anger building up inside her.

'Oh, what rudeness!' Mr Mildew placed a hand on his head, as if he was about to faint. 'If you use any bad language I will have to report you to the village Courtesy Committee.'

The group surrounding the vicar were tutting and shaking their heads, mumbling in agreement. Emilia's face turned purple and Kallie seized her arm in warning. They couldn't afford to get into any more trouble.

'She didn't mean to be rude.' Kallie suddenly found herself speaking; everyone's eyes turned to her. 'I know you don't like us performing Ellsabet's play but have you ever thought that opening up the theatre might bring some good to Merricombe? Theatre should bring people together. That's why I love it. I wouldn't have this chance to be in a real play if it wasn't for Jackie and the Wildstormers . . .'

The group were quiet now. The vicar smiled encouragingly.

'The magic of theatre is . . . is it helps us dream as one,' said Kallie, echoing the words Ellsabet had said to Rose in her letter. 'So you should support it. Instead of believing all these made-up stories about Wildstorm being bad for Merricombe.'

'What sugary sentiment,' sneered Mr Mildew. 'You can't fool us. The Wildstorm Theatre Camp is bad news. And I shall say as much at the village meeting on Friday night. Many in Merricombe have some very strong opinions on the subject. Perhaps it is unwise for Wildstorm to continue—'

'You can't stop us!' growled Emilia. 'We'll show you!' She turned on her heel and marched away.

Kallie hurried after her, glancing back at Mr Mildew, who stood staring after them. Beside him, the vicar still held the poster, looking confused. Something had shifted in the villagers' attitude to Ellsabet. Surely if they were capable of making Ellsabet pastries and paintings, they'd have relished the chance to see her play performed – hadn't Emilia said Ellsabet was like a celebrity to the villagers? Yet now they were full of real fear and suspicion. Kallie remembered Mr Dixson, how a few days ago he'd been singing their praises and today thought them 'theatre ruffians'. Something had changed in Merricombe over these last few days. Kallie felt a chill crawl up her spine.

'Slow down – it's them,' hissed Kallie, catching up with Emilia.

The three Enchanted boys were walking ahead of

them. One by one, the boys climbed over a stile into a meadow and disappeared. Emilia put on a spurt of speed and Kallie had to run to keep up with her.

'Em, what are you doing?'

'Getting to the bottom of this,' said Emilia, her cheeks flushed. 'Mr Mildew makes me mad! It's like nothing has changed in hundreds of years – this village hates anything new and different! They hate Mum and the theatre just like they hated Ellsabet. Well, I won't let them or a bunch of Enchanted kids stop Wildstorm!'

They reached the stile. Beyond it, the boys were walking slowly away across the meadow.

'Hang on,' said Kallie, 'what's your plan? The Enchanted could be dangerous – we don't even know who's behind them yet.'

'Well, it's time to find out, then!' said Emilia, her eyes fixed on Arley's back. 'They might just lead us to some answers.'

Chapter Nineteen

The sun was high but the wood that wrapped around Fallow Hill was strangely dark. It was late afternoon as Kallie and Emilia followed the Enchanted boys into the trees. Kallie felt fear pulsing through her as the shadows closed in around them. Kallie knew Emilia was upset about Arley – but if their theory was correct, he wasn't Arley any more. Kallie tugged Emilia's arm to slow her down.

'Em, we need to be careful.'

'We'll be careful,' said Emilia. 'We're just going to follow them and see where they go. They might lead us to the man who's enchanting them.'

'But we don't know anything about him!' warned Kallie. 'We need to think about this—'

'I'm done thinking about things,' said Emilia sharply.

In the distance, the three boys walked on like soldiers, in silence.

'Emilia! It's dangerous.' Kallie spoke so firmly, Emilia

finally slowed. 'There's something dark going on. This could be a trap!'

Emilia's determined frown faded a little.

'We'll keep our eyes open,' she said.

'I wasn't planning on walking around with my eyes closed!' said Kallie, exasperated. 'Just be careful. Let's follow them but go quietly.'

They climbed uphill, moving cautiously from tree to tree, keeping the boys within their sights. This part of the wood was ancient with gnarled roots like huge tentacles; wispy curtains of ivy cascaded from the arms of grand oaks. Kallie couldn't tell if the boys knew they were being followed. Each time they'd seen them over the last few days, they'd become less and less normal. A thicket of thorns held up their progress and when they emerged on the other side, the boys had vanished.

'Let's keep going this way,' said Kallie. 'I think they were heading for the hilltop.'

A stream now blocked their path, the water rushing over sharp, moss-capped rocks.

'There's a bridge up there' – Emilia pointed – 'or we can take a shortcut over that log,' she added with a grimace.

'No thanks.' Kallie winced, eyeing the flimsy stick that had fallen between the banks. 'I don't fancy ending up in the water.'

As Kallie placed her foot on the little bridge, she heard something. A creak and a snap. Emilia had heard it too and stiffened.

'What was that?'

'There's someone behind us,' whispered Kallie.

Her legs felt weak and the hairs on her arms were standing on end. Another creak – something was definitely creeping up behind them. Kallie swallowed. This had been a very bad idea.

'Turn on three,' muttered Emilia. 'Ready? One. Two. Three!'

They spun around and were greeted by a high-pitched yelp as Marlow Lee leapt in shock.

'What the hell are you doing here?' snarled Emilia.

Marlow gave a sulky shrug. 'I can go for a walk if I want; it's a free country.'

'You were following us,' said Kallie; her heart was still pounding painfully in her chest.

'Oh, what if I was, cheat?' sneered Marlow. 'I know it was because of you two the costumes got stolen. The others are saying you left some back door open but for all we know you stole them yourself.'

'Why would we steal—' Emilia was puffing up like an angry peacock.

'Keep your voice down!' hissed Kallie urgently. 'They'll hear us! Come on – we need to catch them.'

Marlow's presence had given Kallie renewed energy. She was tired of people thinking she was in the wrong. Emilia was right; it was time to get some answers. She led them over the bridge and continued uphill, Marlow and Emilia beside her, squabbling in whispers.

'You really think I'd want to mess up Wildstorm?'

'Well, you're up to something—'

'Just go away! No one wants you here!'

'Quiet!' Kallie held out an arm.

They'd reached the edge of the woods and ahead was the circle of trees surrounding the blackthorn stump. And around the stump stood five people. Not just the three boys; there were two teenage girls standing beside them, blank-eyed and staring. Five Enchanted victims.

'What's that on the ground?' whispered Emilia.

Kallie squinted and saw two huge bin bags; a velvet sleeve was dangling out of one of the bags.

'It's the stolen costumes,' cried Kallie, trying to keep her voice low.

'Those monsters!' snarled Marlow at her shoulder. 'Well, let's go and get them!'

But then the chanting started.

'*Ellsabet . . . Ellsabet . . . Ellsabet . . .*'

Kallie looked quickly at Emilia and it was clear that this time she could hear it too. Her eyes were huge, the fear inside Kallie showing on her friend's face.

'Maybe this wasn't such a good idea,' croaked Emilia. 'I'm sorry. We should go before they notice—'

But Marlow had let out a terrified scream, turned and run back down the hill. Kallie's head whipped back to the Enchanted; there was no way they hadn't heard that. But they were all standing, staring straight ahead, saying Ellsabet's name again and again.

'I think they're sort of on time out,' muttered Kallie, her heart racing, 'waiting for new orders.'

She looked at Emilia, Marlow's shrieks still echoing in the distance.

'Oh no. You're not suggesting what I think you are?' said Emilia.

'If we just walk up and take the stuff, maybe they won't do anything,' said Kallie. The sight of the stolen costumes was too much to bear. They had to do something.

'OK,' agreed Emilia, 'but let's go together.'

Slowly as they could, both of them crept up the slope and stepped into the clearing. The Enchanted didn't look up. Kallie was shaking so much she could hardly breathe. But the costumes were only feet from them. Kallie took another step forward. At this angle, she noticed with a jolt of shock that all of their eyes were closed. She was close enough to see the tattoos on their arms. The inky C had changed; now it looked like a backwards D with the centre shaded in. And the symbol on every wrist was the same. Kallie took another step and reached the costumes, Emilia right behind her. There was a third, smaller bag too. It was full of books and Kallie recognised the title on top – *Posies and Poisons: Good Luck Charms in 16th-Century Britain* – as one of the stolen books from the Historical Society.

Kallie signalled to Emilia and slowly they picked up the bags of costumes. No one moved.

'It's worked,' whispered Kallie, hardly daring to believe it. She slung the book bag over her shoulder. 'All right. Let's get – Emilia! No!'

But Emilia had stepped right up to Arley; his eyes were closed like the others.

'Arley, it's me, Em. Can you hear me? I know you're still in there. I know—'

Kallie knew what she was going to do and cried out a warning – but it was too late. Emilia placed a hand on her old friend's shoulder and at once the boy's eyes snapped open. The chanting stopped.

'Emilia! Run!' shouted Kallie, lifting the bags in her arms.

The Enchanted moved slowly at first, as if groggy, but within seconds they were fully awake and their pounding footsteps were hot on Kallie's heels. She looked around for Emilia and saw her darting through the trees to her right, clutching a bag of costumes to her chest.

Kallie leapt over roots and swerved trees, trying not to think about what would happen if they got caught. Would they be dragged back and shoved into the bags as well? Would they become enchanted too? There would be no pleading with them. These kids weren't thinking for themselves. They were following orders from their unseen master.

As Kallie raced through a patch of nettles – her heart thudding in her ears – she had a sudden idea.

'Emilia! This way!' she yelled and started running in a diagonal.

Behind her she heard the Enchanted's footsteps following her, swerving this way and that as she zigzagged through the woods. She felt a thrill of triumph.

'What are you doing!? They'll catch you!' Emilia shouted, appearing at Kallie's side.

'Just follow me! And get to the stream!' Kallie called.

She swerved and heard their quarry swerve too – the Enchanted were copying their every move, just as Kallie had hoped. The stream came suddenly into view and Kallie pushed Emilia ahead of her.

'Climb over the log – go!'

Emilia hesitated for a second, before stepping on to the log, which swayed dangerously. Kallie made to follow but a hand grabbed her arm; one of the Enchanted girls had her in a pincered grip. Kallie yanked herself free and felt the bag of books slip off her arm – but she held fast to the costumes and began to make her way across the log. It was barely wide enough for her to place one foot in front of the other. The stream rushed below her. She wobbled and felt the log twist beneath her. Two of the Enchanted had followed them on to the log – which shuddered beneath their collective weight. Gritting her teeth, Kallie forced herself to keep moving – one foot at a time. Emilia had reached the far bank and was shouting encouragement. Two more steps. Kallie slipped but Emilia had grabbed her hand and Kallie leapt on to dry land, her bag of costumes spilling out on the grass.

'Quick! Help me!' Kallie cried, pushing at the log with all her might.

They strained together and the log began to slip.

One Enchanted girl had almost reached them and she snatched at Kallie's hair as the log jerked and crashed down into the water, taking the Enchanted with it. The stream wasn't deep but the current was strong and the Enchanted kids were struggling to stand. Their comrades on the opposite bank stared back at Kallie and Emilia; one held the bag of books.

'Let's go!' Kallie bent to gather the costumes but there was a shout from behind them.

'What's going on here?'

Kallie looked up to see Jackie, Violet and Mr Mildew striding through the woods towards them. Behind them trailed a few Wildstormers, including Marlow. The Enchanted turned as one to make their escape. The ones in the water waded to the far bank and clawed their way up on to the grass before running off. Jackie shouted after them.

'Who was that? Was that Arley? I'll want to speak to their parents!' Jackie rounded on Mr Mildew. 'I want those children's names.'

'What a mess!' said Mr Mildew, smirking as he leant on his cane, looking around at the dirty costumes strewn on the grass. 'I hope none of these items are historical. The villagers will want to hear about this at the meeting on Friday.'

'Nothing a good scrub won't sort,' said Violet, starting to bundle the costumes back into the bag. She reached out and gripped Kallie's shoulder. 'Are you OK, love? Did they hurt you?'

'We're – we're OK,' panted Kallie, looking over at Emilia, who had sunk to the ground to catch her breath.

'What happened?' Jackie demanded, looking between Kallie and Emilia. 'Marlow said the village kids were playing some kind of joke?'

With the smallest shake of her head, Emilia told Kallie not to mention anything out of the ordinary.

'They were just messing around,' said Kallie. 'We followed them and found the costumes.'

'A good thing too!' added Violet.

'It seems that the play is saved after all,' said Mr Mildew, sour as grapes. 'For now . . .'

The Wildstormers went to help Violet, a few cheering as they found their own costumes in the stolen loot. In the commotion, something caught Kallie's eye. Poking out of a hole in a tattered skirt was a sheet of paper scribbled with green ink: she knew that handwriting. Kallie took a step towards it but Marlow saw her, and swooped down, stuffing it into his pocket. Kallie dodged around Mr Mildew and collided with Jackie. Marlow slipped away into the crowd, smirking back at her.

'It seems you have righted your wrongs, Kallie,' said Jackie with a thin smile. She looked over at the head of the Historical Society. 'Mr Mildew, this is a theatre matter. The Wildstormers can deal with this alone. I suggest you leave.'

Mr Mildew spun on his heel and marched away, knocking into Kallie as he went but she didn't care. Her stomach bubbled angrily: Marlow had got the second half of Rose Graveheart's letter.

CHAPTER TWENTY

Marlow seemed to have decided that what he'd seen on Fallow Hill had been an elaborate joke cooked up by Kallie and Emilia. Kallie didn't know how he could be so stupid. At Thursday breakfast, he was dealing with the situation by being even louder and more annoying than usual. Kallie and Emilia watched him from over their steaming bowls of porridge.

'We've got to get that letter,' whispered Kallie.

'I just hope he hasn't thrown it away,' said Emilia darkly.

'I think he'll want to keep hold of it to mess with us,' replied Kallie.

'Sounds like Marlow's style,' agreed Emilia, upturning a jar of honey on to her porridge.

Kallie rubbed her eyes. She'd had bad dreams again. One dream had been particularly strange. She'd been in the theatre on the empty stage, facing the Enchanted lolloping towards her. But Kallie hadn't been alone.

Emilia had been standing beside her – but then Emilia had transformed into a stranger with long dark hair and sharp eyes: Ellsabet. She had been trying to tell Kallie something but the words were all mixed up and unfamiliar – Kallie didn't understand what she needed to do. And just as the Enchanted reached the stage, Kallie woke up, muddled and sweating, with her sleeping bag all twisted.

Maybe it had been Kallie's subconscious coaxing her onwards to uncover Ellsabet's story. It made sense for Emilia to turn into Ellsabet – for it felt to Kallie as if Ellsabet was an old friend she'd known long ago. Now Kallie knew who Ellsabet had been, she felt a duty to get to the bottom of this mystery. But most of all they needed to help the Enchanted – before even more joined their ranks. Kallie had to know what Ellsabet's old foe had wanted. Only then could they solve the mystery facing the present-day Merricombe.

'Did you see their tattoos had changed?' said Kallie, keeping her voice low. 'I wish we knew what that's all about. It doesn't even look like a C now.'

'Do you think he was watching us yesterday?' And Kallie knew she meant the unknown villain. 'If he was, why didn't he stop the Enchanted following us on to the log? Why didn't he make them take the bridge?'

'You're right.' Kallie paused. 'If he had been watching us, he'd have given them new orders. So maybe he isn't hiding in the woods any more.'

Kallie couldn't help a shiver pass over her. If he wasn't in the woods, he could be anywhere.

After breakfast, there was the usual charge to the theatre for the morning rehearsal. They were doing their first full costume rehearsal that day. The rest of the cast had been inspired by the return of the costumes and everyone was being much nicer towards Kallie and Emilia, despite Marlow's best efforts to convince everyone it had been their fault the costumes had gone missing.

As Kallie passed by Hollowstar House, she admired the faded symbols as usual. She supposed they'd been there in Ellsabet's time, when the place had been called Moss Cottage. Its connection to Ellsabet made her feel even fonder of the house, as if they now shared a secret together. As she stared at the starry curtains in the lower windows, Kallie was struck by a thought.

'Emilia, they're moons! The tattoos on the Enchanted wrists are the Hay Moon. At first it was just a C like the very thinnest moon crescent,' explained Kallie feverishly. 'But yesterday they were half circles – like half moons.'

'So what does it mean?' said Emilia, fascinated.

'It means time is running out,' said Kallie. 'We need to get the second half of Rose's letter by any means possible before the Hay Moon is full.'

It was a difficult morning. The rehearsal was full of forgotten lines and people blundering onstage before their cue – but on the whole Jackie and Violet were pleased with their progress. It was two days until the show and that also meant it was two days until the Hay Moon. Kallie was so impressed at how far they'd all come in only a few days. Everyone agreed that Emilia made a terrific Storyteller and there was a hushed silence during her speeches. Marlow was very convincing as the evil King, but Kallie privately thought he didn't need to try very hard.

Jackie was working them flat out and Kallie and Emilia didn't have a moment to sneak away to discuss their plans. Kallie often thought Jackie was deliberately keeping an eye on them, preventing them from doing any more 'exploring'.

Kallie couldn't concentrate; her eyes kept sliding to Marlow. How could he be so annoying? He had no idea what he was risking keeping that letter from them – Merricombe was in danger, Kallie knew it.

She was only momentarily distracted when Violet

brought out a box full of coloured sticks – the so-called 'pyrotechnics' Marlow had been going on about. The cast gasped as Violet pulled the string on one of the cylinders and a cloud of red smoke billowed upwards.

'We'll be using these smoke flares for the final battle scene,' explained Violet, after the smoke had wafted away out of the open door, 'but I want everyone to be careful. These are not toys and anyone caught playing with them will be in serious trouble.'

Marlow and his friends were still exclaiming over the smoke flares when Kallie and Emilia hurried off to dinner. They had gobbled down their vegetable lasagne and garlic bread before Marlow had even sat down. They slipped down to the campsite and Emilia snuck into Marlow's tent (which was the large bell-tent he shared with his friends) while Kallie kept watch. But Emilia crawled out empty-handed.

'I bet he's got it in his pocket,' said Kallie, as they slumped against her tent. 'Nothing we can do if he does . . .'

'We could steal his trousers,' Emilia suggested unenthusiastically.

Kallie could barely muster a laugh.

'We should probably practise our lines,' she said with a sigh.

They spent the next few hours testing each other on their parts and Kallie fell asleep exhausted and helpless.

They were proved right at breakfast the next day, when Marlow started fanning himself with the letter, pretending to be overcome by the morning sun. Kallie squeezed her fists as she watched the letter floating dangerously close to Marlow's orange juice, before he stuffed it back into his pocket.

'The selfish twit!' Emilia growled.

It was the day before the play. They didn't need the *1 DAY TO GO* page on the countdown to remind them. Everyone had their scripts next to their breakfast sandwiches, re-reading their lines and muttering them into their mugs of tea. When the cast arrived in the theatre that morning, they found Violet standing next to a rack of thin swords. Everyone crowded in excitedly.

'A special delivery has just arrived.' Violet smiled. 'We will be using these swords for the battle scenes. They've got rubber tips but they can still be dangerous. So if you dare touch them without an adult present, I'll chop your hand off! Now everyone put on these protective jackets and get into pairs and we'll have a practice.'

'Be careful.' Marlow had popped up behind Kallie. 'This is something you're not going to be able to fake.'

Kallie spun to face him.

'I'll fight you,' she said, a lot louder than she'd meant to, and people looked around curiously. 'I mean, I'll pair with you.'

Marlow snorted.

'I don't think you want to fight me,' he said, but she had a feeling he was bluffing.

'Too scared of being a loser?' said Emilia and a few people giggled.

'Fine. But I warned you,' said Marlow, flipping back his hair.

'If I win, you give me the letter you took,' said Kallie quietly.

Marlow pulled out Rose's letter and waved it around as if goading a cat.

'This boring old thing?' he said. 'All right then, but if you lose, I'm feeding it to a sheep.'

Violet clapped for quiet and started handing out swords.

'There are no winners or losers,' she said, with a meaningful look at Kallie and Marlow. 'We're just going to do a few simple moves.'

But Kallie already knew the simple moves. She hadn't

had any formal lessons but she'd become quite obsessed with those stage combat videos for a while. Kallie caught Emilia's eye and her friend grinned.

'Ready!' called Violet. 'Now on the count of—'

But Marlow had already lunged at Kallie, who parried away his advance and stepped backwards. He lunged again and she swept his blade aside easily. He might be the more aggressive competitor but he clearly had no idea what he was doing. Kallie saw a weak point and advanced, pressing him back.

People were moving out of their way, making a space for them in the centre of the auditorium. Violet was hovering around them, shouting, 'Can we please get back to the simple moves!' and Kallie could hear Emilia whooping her support.

She advanced again – Marlow tried to whack her sword away but she darted out of reach then lunged forward, making him stumble backwards. *Advance on the right, weight on the left.* Kallie drove him back again – there was obvious panic on Marlow's red face now as his back hit the wall. Kallie flicked her wrist, knocking Marlow's sword out of his hand. The crowd broke into shocked applause.

'I believe I'll have that letter now, thanks,' said Kallie, handing back Marlow's sword.

Marlow crumpled it into her hand and flounced out of the theatre. Kallie's heart soared, the letter clutched in her fist; they were one step closer to solving this mystery and teaching Marlow a lesson along the way was just a perk of their victory! Kallie turned around, looking for Emilia but she couldn't see her. There was a huddle over by the stage and Kallie rushed to join them.

'What's happened?'

'Everyone keep calm!' Violet looked panicked. 'Make some space, please.'

Emilia was lying, white-faced and eyes closed, on the theatre floor.

CHAPTER TWENTY-ONE

The sunny afternoon had turned stormy. Hard drops of rain pummelled the flowerbeds and the canopy covering the tables. The sky was swirling with clouds and there was a metallic taste of thunder in the air.

Kallie held tight to two plates of pizza as she climbed the crooked staircase at Hollowstar House. Emilia had come round after a minute and Violet had helped her sit up very slowly. Violet said she must be suffering from the heat and Jackie tutted that Emilia needed to watch her blood sugar – and Emilia was bundled up to her bedroom.

Kallie had been left to partner with Ivan. Ivan was a little slow at first – 'This sword is heavy, isn't it!' he moaned – but by the end of the session, with Kallie's encouragement, he was doing all right and even managed to tap Kallie on the toe. But this was mainly because he'd dropped the sword out of exhaustion.

Kallie paused on the first landing, readjusting the pizzas. She'd been allowed to have dinner with Emilia in her room, as long as she didn't stay too long. Hollowstar House was crumbling and peculiar but it was also homely, the kind of home where you ate buttered toast by a crackling fire. Kallie had already spotted several spots perfect for curling up with a notebook. She could imagine Ellsabet sitting in the window seat or the nook under the stairs, avidly writing her play.

As Kallie reached the first landing, she heard someone talking. She paused, the stairs squeaking below her feet.

'. . . is it right to carry on? After everything that has happened?' It was Violet's voice; she sounded exasperated.

'They will not stop this play!' Jackie, authoritative as ever. 'These children are performing tomorrow evening even if I have to put on a ruff and join them onstage myself!'

'But Emilia—'

'She'll be fine! She needs a chocolate biscuit and a good night's sleep.'

'But what if we're doing the wrong thing?' Violet sounded almost scared. 'What if it's true? All

156

those things they're saying in the village about the – the curse.'

'Violet, don't be ridiculous. We are putting on this play.' Jackie's voice rose. 'And that is exactly what I will tell those idiots at the village meeting tonight. They've always been against us! The vicar has disliked me ever since I was child!'

'I thought you said the vicar was an old friend. Have you forgotten how kind he's been—'

'Violet, the villagers are all small-minded buffoons – and no one is going to change my mind on the subject!'

Kallie wanted to hear more but one of the plates slipped and she only just managed to stop it from falling, making such a commotion that she was sure Jackie and Violet had heard her. Before she was discovered snooping, Kallie hurried on upstairs to Emilia's attic bedroom.

Her friend was wrapped up in her duvet, looking pale, but perked up as Kallie squeezed inside.

'Is that pepperoni pizza?'

Smudge, who was curled up on Emilia's bed, looked up too.

'Pepperoni and ham,' said Kallie, passing over the plate. 'I've got mushrooms.'

'Tough luck, mate!' Emilia grinned, already chomping on a slice.

Kallie actually quite liked mushrooms. She sat down on a chair next to the bed to eat. One of the tiny windows was open and the hot breeze ruffled her hair. The rain pattered outside. She was still thinking about what she'd overheard. It wasn't surprising that Jackie was set on doing the play no matter what. But it was what Violet had said about Jackie forgetting about the vicar's kindness. It sounded like Jackie had been caught up in the same blind dislike as the villagers. Where was all this hatred coming from? Kallie wasn't sure if she should mention this to Emilia; besides, they had more important things to be getting on with right now. The second half of Rose Graveheart's letter.

'You feeling all right?' said Kallie, fetching the letter from her pocket.

'Yeah.' Emilia shrugged. 'Got an awful headache – like someone's banging a tin drum in my head.'

'Did anything happen right before you fainted?'

'Well, you were kicking Marlow's butt all around the theatre.' Emilia grinned. 'Then I just blacked out.'

'So you didn't see anything or hear anything?'

'No. It was just the heat,' said Emilia, brushing pizza crumbs off her bed and picking up the letter.

'Shall I read it, then?'

Kallie nodded eagerly and sat back in her chair, chewing her pizza and gazing up at the sloped ceiling. Emilia read aloud:

He will be strongest at the Hay Moon, she told me, for he was no human man. His strength would only grow. He was a creature to be feared. A master of disguise. She called him the Wrathlok.

As we huddled inside Moss Cottage, a summer storm crackling on the horizon, Ellsabet told me the tale of the Wrathlok. John held my hand.

The Wrathlok – a demon of vile cunning – had come from a dark place. An ancient place. Once a year, he would travel to a different village, dressed in a new disguise. He had a talent for stories. Dark stories. Hateful stories. He would whisper them into people's ears. He turned friend against friend, family against family and whole villages against one of their own. His stories made people cruel and fearful. He fed off their pain.

In every village, he would pick a handful of unlucky victims to make his Enchanted. He took their stories - their memories, their dreams, their souls - until they were empty and he could control them like puppets. His Enchanted would do his bidding and help him spread his lies.

Then on the night of the Hay Moon, the Wrathlok would climb to high ground and tell the moon all he had done to torture the village. In return for his tales, the moon made him stronger and gave him the power to make his mischief last for ever. After the Hay Moon, his trickery could never be reversed. His lies would never die. His Enchanted would be silent and empty for ever. And the Wrathlok would be strong enough to roam the land for another year.

That was the disaster that had befallen Ellsabet's village. Ellsabet's father was a butcher and the Wrathlok had whispered to the villagers that he was poisoning their food and he had plans to murder his customers. Ellsabet could not make the villagers – her friends – see sense. They all believed her father guilty. But Ellsabet had kept her mind. The Wrathlok found it harder to break into her thoughts, harder to mislead her with his whispered tales or enchant her mind. For she too had the heart of a Storyteller, just like him – but one who told stories for good. Yet she was unable to save her father and the villagers locked him away. She had no choice but to run.

And now the Wrathlok had come to Merricombe. And he was spinning a new story: the story of Ellsabet the Witch.

I was afraid. My father had become one of the Enchanted. Ellsabet knew them from the mark on their wrists. The mark of the Hay Moon. Once the Hay Moon was full, there would be no return for him, no return for the villagers who had been hoodwinked by the demon's tales.

'I have spoken with many wise scholars,' said Ellsabet. 'There is a way we can defeat him.'

'We must fight it! We must get to Father and shake the demon from his mind!' John cried.

'Brute force will not stop him,' was Ellsabet's reply. 'I have been learning how we may use stories for good, while he uses them for ill. In the end, we must defeat him with the quill.'

My brother was desperate to fight but Ellsabet begged us both to stay in Moss Cottage. But John would not be contained. He ventured out into the dark night and he did not return. Next morning, I saw him in the village, staring at nothing. Enchanted like Father.

Ellsabet's heart broke. I watched with tears as she found John and Father and, using her own stories to coax and soothe them, she brought them to the theatre. Her words seemed to ease the enchantment but any moment they might turn on us like rabid dogs. We locked them inside the theatre.

'We must call the players together,' announced Ellsabet. 'We must continue with The King's Downfall – tonight!'

But no players came. No actors braved the stage. No audience assembled to watch. Ellsabet paced back and forth, in a fever of her thoughts. I watched her in helpless fear.

'We must run!' I warned her, for the Hay Moon was fast approaching. 'It's our only hope.'

'No! He will come for me, Rose.' She spoke calmly but her eyes darted like two rabbits. 'I am going to try to stop him but I cannot destroy him for ever. He will return.' She pressed her playscript into my arms. 'You must keep this play safe, Rose. The play holds the answer. One day a successor of my heart – a new Storyteller – will come to Merricombe and they must use the play to defeat him.'

Before I could answer, the theatre doors were blown wide – he stood there, the Wrathlok, with a smile to haunt my dreams. He had not yet transformed into his true form, for the Hay Moon was not yet high, but his disguise could not hide his demonic soul.

Ellsabet spoke – I recognised her words from her play – and he roared and moaned and all of a sudden he wilted like a dead weed. Like a cloud of shadows, he fled through the open door and away into the forest.

Before I could rejoice, I saw the villagers – marching towards us, brandishing flaming sticks and hurtful cries. I ran to Ellsabet's side.

'I have weakened him,' she gasped, 'but his stories and lies are still poisoning the villagers' minds. They have come for me. They have come for the witch! You must hide! You must keep my story safe, Rose. He may not return for many hundreds of years but he will return and he must be defeated.'

'I won't let them take you!'

'You must keep my story safe for my successor.' Ellsabet seized my hand. 'They will have the voice to stop him!' The villagers were nearly upon us. 'I trust you, Rose. My best friend.'

We had no time to say goodbye – the villagers stormed the theatre, familiar faces turned ugly with fear, and they dragged Ellsabet away. Some snatched at the playscript and I fought them off – but one page was torn from my grasp. They blamed Ellsabet *for all that was wrong in the village and as the moon rose – white as bone – they burnt her on Fallow Hill.*

With the Wrathlok gone, the Enchanted awoke with no memory of their imprisonment. Ellsabet had saved them. My brother John and father were themselves again. But the bad feeling in the village remained. It seemed even though the demon had vanished, his cruel stories lived on in the villagers' heads.

Merricombe is no longer my home and it is with a heavy heart that I leave for new adventures. I leave this letter in the theatre, which John built and Ellsabet dreamt of, for the successor of Ellsabet Graveheart, in the hope that one day, Ellsabet's story will help you.

For one hot summer the demon will return. You must find the play, take up Ellsabet's fight and you must defeat him once and for all.

Yours in love,

Rose Graveheart

Kallie and Emilia sat in silence. Outside, the rain jabbed lightly at the windowpane. In the garden below, the chatter of their fellow Wildstormers sounded distant and unworldly.

'It's . . . he's a demon?' croaked Kallie.

Her heart was hammering inside her chest. Everything around her felt blurred and strange as if the bedroom might melt away into smoke.

'And he's back,' said Emilia slowly.

'And there's only one person who can stop him,' whispered Kallie. 'The successor of Ellsabet Graveheart.'

Everything was slotting into place. Hollowstar House had been passed down through generations of families . . . from Gravehearts to Masters . . . but what if they had only ever been one family? Kallie looked up at Emilia. She remembered the way the Enchanted had moved towards Emilia on the hilltop, the way they had all burst into life at Emilia's touch. She remembered the dream in which Emilia had turned into Ellsabet. There could only be one explanation. Kallie knew there wasn't time to be afraid any more, because she needed to be there for her friend.

'Ellsabet must have had a child,' said Kallie with a shuddering breath. 'The successor of Ellsabet Graveheart. The person who can destroy the Wrathlok. Emilia, it's you.'

But Emilia was shaking her head. Kallie stared at her, confused.

'But your family own the theatre – the house –

they've owned it for ages. Your mum is from Merricombe. You must be related to the Gravehearts, you—'

'No, Kallie. I knew you'd say that' – Emilia gave a little smile – 'but it's not me. You see . . . I'm adopted.'

CHAPTER TWENTY-TWO

The rain thudded on the roof and echoed strangely in Kallie's head. She hadn't been expecting that.

'Mum can't have kids so she got me,' said Emilia, with a shrug. 'I was just a baby so I never got to know my birth parents. I'm not that interested in them, frankly. I've got Mum and that's all that matters. Oh, and Violet and Smudge too, of course.'

'But without the successor,' Kallie gasped, 'there's nothing we can do to stop the Wrathlok. Arley and the other Enchanted will never be saved. They'll be empty for ever.'

Cold dread was freezing Kallie's heart. There was nothing they could do to help.

'Ellsabet never had a child,' said Emilia softly. 'Rose would have mentioned a baby in the letter. But blood isn't the only bond that counts – look at me and Mum!'

'But then if they're not related by blood, the successor could be anyone. How are we going to find them?!'

cried Kallie, but Emilia was smiling.

'I think it's obvious who the successor is here,' said Emilia. 'It's you, Kallie. You're the hero who's going to defeat this demon! You're the new Storyteller of Merricombe.'

Kallie sat back; her pizza crust slipped to the floor. No, this wasn't how things worked out. She wasn't the hero. Kallie had never been the hero. She wanted to write heroic characters. She didn't want to *be* one.

'I think there might be a mistake,' Kallie began.

'Oh no!' Emilia was beaming now. 'You've been having weird dreams since you arrived – you knew the story of the play before we even read it!'

'But . . . but you didn't hear the Enchanted saying Ellsabet's name during the challenge.'

Emilia shrugged; she was still grinning.

'I think I heard something but I didn't want to admit it in front of Marlow; I didn't want to believe something spooky was happening! But you knew something strange was going on with those village kids. And the quill!' Emilia was almost shouting with excitement. 'You've been dreaming about Ellsabet's green quill. You're connected to her. You're a storyteller – a great playwright like Ellsabet!'

Kallie felt her chest growing tight.

'But how do you know?' she stuttered. 'How is this possible?'

'Kallie, sometimes there are bonds we can't see,' Emilia said. 'Storytelling isn't in your blood, it's in your soul – or your mind – or wherever it comes from! You are Ellsabet's successor. Ellsabet knew you'd come to Merricombe – to finish what she started – to finish the Wrathlok!'

'But I can't defeat a demon,' said Kallie weakly. 'We don't even know what he is exactly.'

Behind her, the open window rattled on its hinges. Emilia picked up the letter and studied it.

'He's . . . "*A creature to be feared. A master of disguise*",' she read, consulting the letter. 'He makes up stories and puts them in people's heads. Oh, and he enchants some people and takes away their souls. The Hay Moon makes him stronger and makes all his tricks last for ever. Blimey! A demon *is* worse than a witch.'

'He must be the reason the villagers suddenly hate Wildstorm,' muttered Kallie, fiddling with her hair. 'Just like he made up that stuff about Ellsabet and her father, he's been spreading bad stories around the village—'

'Well, Mr Mildew was already an evil busybody so it

wouldn't be hard to convince him,' huffed Emilia.

'Maybe it's not just the villagers he's getting to,' said Kallie thoughtfully. 'I heard your mum and Violet talking. Jackie thinks everyone in the village is against Wildstorm; she's forgotten how they helped Wildstorm last year. That's what he does – he divides people! Only this time he might be weaker – because of what Ellsabet did to him.'

'Is Mum OK?' Emilia gulped. 'She's not been enchanted, has she?'

'No, don't worry. He only enchants a few people to be his servants. A handful of unlucky victims,' said Kallie bitterly. 'He keeps the others human enough to mess around with. "*He fed off their pain*" – that's what Rose said, right?'

'How does he do it?' Emilia looked scared. 'How does he whisper bad stories? Do they just travel on the air or something?'

'I dunno.'

They both fell silent. Both lost in the darkest corners of their imaginations.

'The Wrathlok,' muttered Kallie. The name was dark and deadly, like the deep beat of a drum. 'How am I supposed to stop him?'

'Well, you won't be doing it alone, that's for sure,'

said Emilia, with the tone of someone pulling herself together. 'You might be the successor but I'm here too. We'll figure it out together.'

She said it as easily as if she was offering to join Kallie for a spot of pudding, rather than face unknowable dangers together! Kallie felt the tightness in her chest ease very slightly. They both looked back to the letter.

'So how do we stop him?' said Emilia.

'We need to find him first,' said Kallie, moving to sit on the edge of the bed. 'Rose never says what he disguises himself as.'

'So he could be anything!' said Emilia. 'He could be a cat! Oh blimey, I hope it's not Smudge.'

Smudge was still snoozing on Emilia's bed. He opened one eye and gave them a disapproving look before closing it again.

'I don't think so,' said Kallie. 'Ellsabet says some words from the play to stop him – it must be a . . . a spell.'

Kallie couldn't think of another word for it.

'Rose says "*use the play*",' said Emilia, nodding. 'Ellsabet must have hidden the words to the spell in the play.'

'Yes.' Kallie grinned. 'The story in the play is kind of like Ellsabet's story, isn't it? The Storyteller escapes the evil North King and he chases her across the lands, rescued by the Southern Lord and his son. So the King is meant to be the Wrathlok. And the Southern Lord is like Rose and John's father.'

'Let's find this spell, then!' said Emilia, pulling her script on to her lap.

They flicked through the script but they knew it well enough from rehearsals. Kallie turned to the back. Surely it would be around the moment the King was defeated in the story. The final scene was a furious battle between the King's Courtiers and the Southern Lord's soldiers, which ended when the North King fell off his horse. In their production, the final scene involved Marlow being lifted up by the King's Courtiers and carried through the air into a blackout.

'You know, I always thought this ending was a bit sudden.' Kallie frowned. 'And it seemed weird that the Storyteller isn't even in the final scene.'

'What if this isn't the final scene?' said Emilia. 'Remember, Mum said the play had some parts missing. And look – in the letter, Rose says someone snatched a page out of her hand. So what if the real final scene is lost?'

'That must be the spell.' Kallie flopped back in her chair. 'What do we do now? Where's the missing script?'

'Could be anywhere,' sighed Emilia. 'Maybe someone else has already found it and sold it to the Historical Society.'

'Oh – wait a moment!' Kallie's mind felt cranky, like a badly wound clock, but slowly it was all beginning to make sense. 'The logbook at the Historical Society . . . MS 1600!'

'What?'

'It was in this logbook in the office,' said Kallie, jumping to her feet. 'Mr Mildew had taken out something called *MS 1600*. MS means manuscript, right?'

'If you say so.' Emilia shrugged.

'So it's a manuscript written in 1600, the same time as Rose's letter – same time as Ellsabet's play. I bet that manuscript is the missing script! Come on! It must be it!' The wind was in her sails now and she was ready for action. 'Where does Mr Mildew live?'

'Um . . . big house called The Ferns. Not too far, but hold on – you're not thinking of breaking in, are you?'

'Yep.' Kallie gave a grim nod.

'Wow! My bad habits are rubbing off on you.' Emilia grinned. 'What happened to the shy playwright I met at the beginning of the week?'

'Well, this is important,' said Kallie. 'There's never been anything more important. It's the Hay Moon

173

tomorrow night – we've got to find the Wrathlok and stop him before he returns to full strength and the Enchanted are stuck and his lies will never be stopped. Let's go tonight, once everyone is asleep.'

Kallie was still terrified but there was a fire inside her now. With Emilia by her side, Kallie felt, in that moment, that there was nothing they couldn't do. Together they were going to defeat a demon.

They thought it best for Kallie to go back to the campsite, calling a loud goodbye to Jackie and Violet on the stairs, and wait a few hours before their siege on The Ferns.

Kallie clutched Emilia's spare key as she returned up the garden path, the contents of Rose's letter still rattling around her mind. The rain had lifted and the dark sky was studded with stars. Kallie tiptoed to the door and listened. Hollowstar House was quiet. Yet as she reached for the handle, she found that the door was unlocked. Perhaps Emilia had left it open for her.

Kallie crept up the creaking stairs. Smudge was pretending to sleep on the landing outside Emilia's bedroom.

'Have they gone?' whispered Kallie, as she shut the bedroom door behind her.

Emilia was dressed in black, like Kallie, resting on the edge of her bed. She still looked a bit pale.

'Yep, they left about half an hour ago for the village meeting,' said Emilia. 'Hopefully Mr Mildew will blabber on for ages so we'll be back before them.'

'We'll be quick.' Kallie nodded; she was straining to be gone.

'Let's go through the kitchen,' added Emilia, as they slunk out of the bedroom.

'Good idea. We'll need supplies,' said Kallie. 'Torches, rope, gloves . . . um . . . a screwdriver?'

If she was honest with herself, Kallie had no idea what would be useful in a break-in.

Emilia kept the lights off so they had to feel their way into the hall. Kallie's eyes were drawn to the black windows; with a shudder, she wondered where the Enchanted were at this moment. What orders they were following tonight. There was a rattling noise and Kallie squinted into the dark corners but saw nothing. Probably just the wind through the walls.

Emilia pushed open the kitchen door; it creaked ominously. The kitchen was full of shadows, pots and pans gleaming like many eyes in the darkness. Yet there was something missing. Kallie frowned as they stepped forward, not speaking. There was a strange absence of grey starlight. It was too dark somehow.

And then Kallie saw him – a figure, outlined against the glass door, loomed above them. Kallie stumbled backwards, fear like a dart in her stomach. As Burn stepped forward, the old cook's face was sunken, his eyes oddly blank, blocking their escape.

Chapter Twenty-Three

He walked swiftly, sheltered by the shadows of the hedges. A fox scampered out of his path and flattened itself into the ditch. He paid it no attention. His mind was focused on the approaching feast: the village meeting. A buffet of high emotions and frustrated feelings. He licked his lips. He could not wait to taste the fear and suspicion that swamped the villagers' minds.

Oh, he was looking forward to the yells and the accusations and the bullying!

'The theatre is bad for the village!'

'The witch will curse us for allowing the play to take place!'

'Merricombe would be better off without your stinking theatre kids!'

He imagined the villagers shouting, red-faced and fretful. Of course, Jackie Masters would come back with a load of huff and puff about the theatre camp being good for the village – good for the children! That would only antagonise the villagers – he would fill their minds with mistrust . . .

He laughed aloud, his voice cutting into the night like an animal bark. Oh, tonight would be a party!

He sniggered as the lights of the village square came into view. He could already see the crowd forming outside the café, where the meeting was being held.

That Ellsabet Graveheart had been a real thorn in his side – and now she would be remembered for ever as a witch, evil to the core. She might have bettered him all those years ago but he was wiser now. His four-hundred-year-long nap had sharpened him. He would not be thwarted by any human again! He would have his fun with the villagers and he would take his revenge on the new Storyteller of Merricombe in Ellsabet's place.

He kept close to the shadows, stalking beside the churchyard wall. He must still be cautious.

As for the two girls, they were no threat to his plans; he had left them in good hands.

Chapter Twenty-Four

The cook was not himself.

Burn's eyes were empty as he stared across the dark kitchen at Kallie and Emilia, who were rooted to the spot. Kallie could feel Emilia trembling beside her. Burn's hand shot out and grabbed a frying pan from the side. He swung it like a club.

'You will not leave,' he croaked; it was Burn's voice but Kallie knew they weren't his words.

Burn might be thin and wiry, but he was armed and they were not. Kallie's eyes darted from the frying pan to the sideboard, to the stacks of drying plates, folded tablecloths and a huge copper pot. Just out of reach.

Burn took a lumbering step towards them, the frying pan raised.

'What do we do?' whispered Emilia. 'Do you think he'd hurt us?'

'He's not in control,' replied Kallie. 'We need to get round him. We need a plan—'

But before either of them could think of one, a shadow streaked between them and pounced at Burn's knees.

'Smudge! No!' Emilia cried, diving after her cat.

Smudge was clawing up Burn's leg and the old man howled, the frying pan waving dangerously close to Emilia's head. Kallie leapt for the sideboard, seized a plate and hurled it across the room at Burn. It hit him on the shoulder and he lurched towards Kallie, Smudge still hanging on to his leg.

Kallie stumbled backwards and knocked into a shelf, toppling mugs, which smashed on the floor. Emilia was crouched down, trying to coax Smudge to safety – Burn kicked out and Emilia keeled backwards. Kallie grabbed a pot and chucked it as hard as she could; it caught Burn's hand and the frying pan soared out of his grip and struck the kitchen clock with a clang.

Kallie grabbed a tablecloth and threw it over the cook's face and shoulders. He blundered around, like some bizarre polka-dot ghost, hitting a drawer and sending cutlery flying. A fork landed with a horrible thud inches from Kallie's hand as she crawled across the floor to Emilia.

'Let's go!' shouted Kallie, and hoisted up her friend. But Burn had thrown off the tablecloth; Smudge was now hanging on to his jumper, yowling like a burglar alarm. Kallie and Emilia braced themselves as the cook jerked towards them – then all of a sudden there was a loud *BONG!* and Burn fell flat on his face and lay still.

Kallie looked around, panting and confused. The light blinked on to reveal Marlow, standing by the door, the frying pan in his hands.

'What – what are you doing?' he stammered.

'What are *you* doing?' retorted Emilia, but her voice was shallow; she sank to the floor, breathing hard.

'Em?' Kallie rushed to her. 'Are you OK? Did he hurt you?'

'Just a bit worn out.' Emilia smiled, her eyes closed. 'Just need to catch my breath.'

'Er . . . are you going to explain why you were having a midnight food fight?' Marlow was gazing around the devastation of the kitchen.

'Thanks for your help but this is private,' said Kallie, bending down to rescue Smudge from under the tablecloth.

Burn was knocked out cold, his eyes closed. Kallie felt his pulse and the back of his head for blood. He seemed all right but he was going to have an awful headache tomorrow.

'Since you're here, would you mind giving me a hand?' Kallie looked at Marlow.

Still gawping, Marlow took Burn's other arm and together they dragged him into the spare bedroom at the back of the kitchen. They struggled to lift him on to the bed and tuck him in. Kallie looked back at him sadly as they closed the door and locked it. So that made six Enchanted victims; how many more had fallen under the Wrathlok's magic?

Back in the kitchen, Kallie looked sharply at Marlow.

'What are you doing here anyway?'

'ME!?' Marlow gaped at her. 'You just knocked out the cook!'

'Actually, you knocked out the cook,' said Kallie, 'and thanks,' she added, reminding herself that Marlow had in fact saved them.

'But *you* were fighting him!' Marlow stared at her. 'What happened, he made you a bad boiled egg?'

'How did you get in?' interrupted Kallie.

'Front door was open.' Marlow shrugged. 'But what's going on?'

'There isn't time!'

Emilia was still on the floor; Smudge sat next to her, purring protectively. Kallie found a washing line – no screwdrivers, but she thought a fork might come in handy. She tried tidying up as best she could but they needed to get going before Jackie and Violet came back from the village meeting. Kallie turned to Emilia.

'How are you feeling?'

Emilia hung her head.

'I think I hit my head again,' Emilia muttered. 'It feels woolly . . . I'm sorry. I don't think I can come.'

'Don't worry,' said Kallie quickly. 'You rest – you'll feel better in the morning.'

'I'll feel better than Burn, that's for sure.'

'Smudge will keep you company,' said Kallie. 'I'll go to The Ferns and find the missing script.'

She turned to the kitchen door but Marlow stepped in front of her.

'I really need to go—' Kallie began but Marlow cut across her.

'You'd better start telling me what's going on,' he said, jutting out his chin, 'because I'm coming with you.'

CHAPTER TWENTY-FIVE

A curtain of stars guided Kallie and Marlow's way down the dark road. The walk to Mr Mildew's house, The Ferns, wasn't far but at night everything felt bigger and wilder. Kallie still felt jumpy after their encounter with the cook.

Were there more of the Enchanted waiting to stop them? Or would the Wrathlok deal with them himself? Had he somehow known that they would try to look for the missing script? thought Kallie. That must mean they were on the right track.

Kallie was listening intently for the smallest sound in the shadows. But the countryside was silent – or at least, it would have been silent if Marlow hadn't been chattering away like a spluttering tap.

'So Ellsabet isn't a witch? And this demon, the Wrathlok thing, is back in Merricombe turning people into zombies?' Marlow gawped. 'And you're like some second Storyteller? Ellsabet the Second?!'

It had been easier to tell him the truth, although he was having trouble swallowing it. To be honest, Kallie couldn't blame him. She felt heavy. Even now she still wondered whether Emilia had made a mistake. Maybe Kallie wasn't the successor. Maybe she was just a girl who liked writing plays and had just happened to stumble upon the mystery of the Wildstorm curse. But then she thought of Arley and Burn, how it would feel to lose who you were – lose your own inner stories – and be empty, to just follow orders. She had to do something to help them. She focused on the night's task: find the missing script – which might or might not contain the answer to defeating the Wrathlok before the Hay Moon.

'And how do we know we won't get caught? How do we know it's safe?' Marlow was still puffing along beside her. 'How do you know you are this successor? How do you—'

'Look!' Kallie turned to him. 'You don't need to come with me. You can go back now. I don't even know why you offered in the first place – I'm not exactly your favourite person.'

Marlow shuffled his shoes.

'I dunno – I thought it sounded like a fun adventure,' he said finally. 'And I knew you two were up to something – always creeping around and whispering together.'

'It's you who's been doing the creeping around – spying on us,' said Kallie. 'Like tonight.'

Marlow shrugged.

'I couldn't sleep, OK? I was thinking about those kids chanting on Fallow Hill,' he mumbled. 'It was so freaky. Then I heard you go past my tent, so I got dressed and followed . . . I just wanted to know what was going on – that letter didn't make any sense. I thought maybe you'd written it.'

'You only read the second half,' pointed out Kallie, 'and if you had just given it back to me in the first place, we'd have more time to work out how to stop the Wrathlok.'

'I'm sorry.' He sounded like he meant it. 'I know I haven't been very nice to you.'

'No, you haven't.'

'Well, I'm honestly sorry.' He blushed. 'I dunno. You turned up out of the blue, winning the playwriting competition and you're instantly best friends with Emilia – and she still thinks I'm this big-headed show-off and you're all super-smart and cool.'

'Wait a moment – are you jealous? Of me?'

'No. Duh!' He rolled his eyes, but it wasn't entirely

186

convincing. 'I just wanted to know what's going on – OK? You two always seem to be having fun.'

Kallie glanced sideways at him. She knew what it felt like to be left out. But she was still surprised to hear this from Marlow Lee, the boy who was always in the centre of the popular crowd.

'Mr Mildew will be at the village meeting tonight,' said Kallie, after an awkward pause. 'We should be able to get in and out before he's back.'

'You know in that letter,' said Marlow cautiously, 'it said this Wrathlok was a master of disguise; you don't think he could be a tree or a plant or something? He could be watching us right now.'

Without wanting to, they both glanced behind them.

'And have you got, you know' – Marlow gave her a wide-eyed stare – 'like, witch's powers and that?'

'Ellsabet wasn't a witch!'

'Yeah, but didn't she do something to John and his father to help them when they were enchanted? Soothe them with her stories, it said.'

'I thought you said the letter was nonsense,' said Kallie, eyebrows raised. 'You certainly gave it a good read.'

They turned a bend and the entrance to The Ferns stood ahead of them, and beyond it a driveway leading away into blackness.

'Look.' Kallie turned to Marlow. 'Thanks for helping us in the kitchen. But you don't need to come—'

'I can help,' he protested. 'I got Jackie and Violet to come and save you from those kids in the wood, didn't I? I've got ideas, I've—'

'I don't know what's going to happen in there,' said Kallie firmly. 'I don't know if we're going to be able to find the script or get caught. I have to try but you don't need to come with me.'

'I'm not scared,' said Marlow, in a high-pitched squeak.

Kallie raised her eyebrows. 'Well, if you're sure. But please don't scream and give us away.'

'I am not a screamer!' Marlow spluttered. 'I just sometimes make the occasional noise when surprised.'

There was nothing else for it. Kallie led the way between the brick pillars. Tall ferns lined the driveway and trimmed lawns yawning into the darkness on either side of them. They walked for at least a minute before they saw the house itself. Grey against the dark sky, it was a mountain of high windows, carved arches and pointed battlements. The stone walls were worn and bruised from centuries of sun and rainfall. Kallie could only marvel at the stories these walls had seen.

'Blimey! Mr Mildew's got his own golfing green,' muttered Marlow, pointing to the flat lawn behind the house, 'and he's got his own golf cart! Maybe he isn't so bad after all . . .'

'We're not here to play golf,' Kallie whispered. 'Please keep quiet.'

The two of them crept around the outside of the house, keeping to the shadows. At the back, they saw a low window. Kallie, who thought she'd had enough of climbing through windows, allowed Marlow to lift her up. The window was a little higher than she'd hoped and she really had to struggle to heave open the pane. She peered inside – it looked like a storeroom. Quietly as she could, she lowered the washing line they'd brought so Marlow could scramble up after her. He fell over the sill with a small thump and Kallie gave him a warning look.

They stood still, listening. They could hear nothing but the distant ticking of a clock.

'Let's find his study,' Kallie mouthed.

The house was even grander inside. Dark wood-panelled corridors were hung with oil paintings depicting ancient manor houses and snooty horses. Kallie was grateful for the thick carpet, which dampened their footsteps.

At each door they came to, Kallie paused and put her ear against it before peering inside. The door handles were stiff and Kallie had to lift them slowly to avoid any creaking. Mr Mildew should be out at the village meeting but they didn't know who else might be here.

At last they found a room that Kallie assumed was Mr Mildew's study. The starlight poured from the curtainless windows on to a huge desk in the centre covered in neat piles of papers, books and a large vase of flowers. There was another door leading into a library beyond. They closed the study door carefully behind them and then switched on their torches.

They set about searching, careful to put everything back exactly as they'd found it. It didn't take long to find what they'd come for. Kallie moved aside a pile of books and underneath there was a box labelled *MS 1600*. It had a flimsy lock on the front but some delicate twisting with the fork and the lock sprang open. Kallie opened it eagerly.

'This is it! It's the missing script!' Kallie's heart swelled with excitement.

She ran a hand over the rough parchment; it was ripped at the edges but the words were still visible. Blotchy, slanting words that Ellsabet had written so many hundreds of years ago, passing on her story through time and history.

Marlow held the torch above her, equally awed. Kallie's heart was beating so hard, the words seemed to vibrate on the page but she took a deep breath and read slowly:

THE STORYTELLER faces THE KING with the full moon behind them.

THE KING has fallen from his horse and lies on the ground.

THE STORYTELLER holds her weapon high.

THE STORYTELLER:
You may choose the face you wear and a voice to match,

Dress up in human skin to suit the plots you hatch,

But I know who you are: a demon amongst men.

Ancient, restless spirit, you will not win again!

> *There is magic in my voice, magic in my quill;*
>
> *With these words, I conquer and overturn your will.*
>
> *So THE STORYTELLER speaks, undoing THE KING's power with her words. THE KING vanishes in a puff of smoke. Never to return again.*

Kallie's heart sang inside her. This was their way to defeat the Wrathlok. The Storyteller's final speech.

'So what does it mean?' said Marlow eagerly at her shoulder.

'I think it's a spell,' said Kallie. 'She says "*There is magic in my voice, magic in my quill*". Don't know what that weapon she's holding is, though. These words must defeat the Wrathlok when the Storyteller says them . . . well . . . um . . . that's me, I guess.'

I hope, she thought privately.

'Why couldn't Ellsabet just *say* that?' grumbled Marlow. 'So now we've got to find this weapon?'

But there was something else nagging in the back of Kallie's mind. *You may choose the face you wear . . . Dress up in human skin . . .* surely that meant the Wrathlok was disguised as a human?

Kallie's eyes swept over the desk and she noticed the titles of the books she'd shoved aside: *Warding Off Evil, Posies and Poisons: Good Luck Charms in 16th-Century Britain, Bad Spirits in Ancient Europe.* She recognised these titles. They had been on the list of stolen items in the Historical Society. She'd seen them with the Enchanted on Fallow Hill. But why would they be here on Mr Mildew's desk? Unless . . .

'I think we made a very big mistake coming here,' whispered Kallie.

It seemed so obvious now. Someone who would do anything to stop the play. Someone who hated the theatre. *A demon amongst men . . .* Hiding in plain sight.

'Mr Mildew.' Kallie's voice was hoarse. 'He's dangerous. I think he's—'

There was a faint crunch of gravel from outside. The study's windows looked directly out on to the driveway and someone was walking towards the house.

Kallie and Marlow looked at each other.

'Let's go!' hissed Marlow.

They flicked off their torches; Kallie grabbed the

script and pelted across the room. Marlow flung the door open and they both screamed.

Arley and another Enchanted boy stood in the doorway, both holding candles like drawn swords. Behind them, down the wide staircase, the front door clicked open and Mr Mildew's cane tapped on the marble floor.

Kallie's stomach dropped with fear. The Wrathlok had arrived.

CHAPTER TWENTY-SIX

The Enchanted boys seized Kallie and Marlow and forced them back into the study. Kallie could feel the heat from the boys' candles as they held them up. Their eyes were foggy. Arley was holding Kallie and she could see the tattoo on his wrist, the inky moon almost full.

Below, in the hallway, Kallie could hear smart shoes and the click of Mr Mildew's cane across the floor. Coming ever closer. Only it wasn't Mr Mildew, she reminded herself. He had been right under their noses the whole time. A demon in disguise. Kallie wondered if the real Mr Mildew was still inside or was the Wrathlok wearing Mr Mildew like a coat? Kallie worked hard not to retch at the thought.

Right now, the details didn't matter. Right now, they needed to get away fast. Kallie didn't want to think about what the Wrathlok would do if he caught them.

'What the hell are we going to do?' gasped Marlow.

'He – he's coming! How're we going to talk our way out of this?'

Kallie felt a rush of inspiration. Something Marlow had said on their walk about Ellsabet soothing John and Rose's father with her stories. She looked up at Arley, his hand tight on her shoulder.

'Arley?' No reaction. 'Arley! He might be controlling you but if you're still in there, then listen, listen with all your strength. I know who you are, Emilia told me about you – about Arley: the boy who loves performing, who loved Wildstorm—'

'What are you doing!?' squeaked Marlow.

Down the corridor, there was the soft thud of Mr Mildew's cane. He had reached the top of the stairs. Kallie kept her eyes fixed on Arley.

'You used to make up songs to learn your lines,' Kallie raced on, 'you and Emilia – do you remember? Trying on hats from the costume box, laughing at Emilia when she wore the one that looked like a chocolate cake—'

The boy's eyes flickered; his mouth twitched. It was such a small movement, Kallie almost missed it. But he'd definitely moved. He was still in there – she knew it!

'You remember Emilia – you were friends!' Kallie

continued, the trudge of feet in the corridor growing louder and louder. 'Last summer, you did a play set under the sea in a huge tent with real seaweed hanging from the roof. Remember Emilia – please!'

Arley was blinking, confused; his hand dropped limply from her shoulder and Kallie wriggled free.

'Quick, do this one!' cried Marlow. The other boy had backed him into the wall and was holding the candle dangerously close to Marlow's cheek.

'There isn't time!' hissed Kallie, looking wildly around for something to help them.

'The flowers!' The voice came from behind her – she turned to see Arley, rubbing his face and looking more like a normal boy than she'd ever seen him.

She seized the vase of flowers and emptied it over the boy holding Marlow. The water extinguished the flame of his candle, but the boy didn't even react – he grabbed Marlow's throat.

'No!' yelled Kallie; in desperation, she swung the vase and it smashed over the boy's head. The boy crumpled and Marlow gasped for breath.

'He's growing stronger,' croaked Arley. They whirled around to face him. He was still blinking dazedly. 'Once the Hay Moon has risen – after sunset tomorrow – he'll have us for ever.'

There was a quickening of footsteps outside.

'It's like a nightmare in my head.' Arley stared desperately at Kallie. 'I can't keep him out for long. Tell Emilia I'm sorry I couldn't come back – I wanted to tell her—'

'He's coming!' cried Kallie, seizing Marlow's arm and pushing him towards the side door to the library. 'Arley! Come with us!'

But the door to the study was opening and Kallie saw Arley's eyes misting over – his whole body straightened up as if pulled by invisible cords and he stared back at her, cold-eyed again.

There wasn't time to waste – Marlow was already sprinting across the library and Kallie slammed the door to the study shut and pelted after him. The two of them burst through another door and found themselves back in the corridor. They raced down it.

'We need to get back to the storeroom,' gasped Marlow, 'before Mr Mildew finds us.'

'It's not Mr Mildew – he's the Wrathlok!' cried Kallie, almost hitting the wall as they swerved a corner. 'The demon! He's in disguise!'

'What? How?'

'I'll explain later!' panted Kallie. She could hear two sets of footsteps running behind them now – Arley and his comrade had resurfaced.

The door to the storeroom was ahead and they barrelled into it, closing the door and shoving whatever they could find to block it: boxes, candlesticks, a broken bookcase. There was a bang – fists pummelled the door.

'It's time to go!' Kallie yanked Marlow to the window and they peered out.

The drop down seemed a lot higher than the climb up. But Kallie forced herself to be calm. She clambered over the sill and began to ease herself down on the washing line as fast as she could. She fell on the stone patio and Marlow dropped beside her and pulled her to her feet.

They left the washing line where it was and ran for the gates, thundering across the lawn. Kallie's chest was screaming in pain, she felt sick, her legs sore – but somehow she kept on running and they made it to the entrance. For a second, she looked back – the lawn and driveway were empty but there was movement in a window of the house. A flame, curling orange in the darkness like an eye watching from a shadowed face.

All seemed quiet when Marlow and Kallie finally reached Hollowstar House. They slipped around the side and prepared to creep across the garden to the campsite. But as they passed the windows of Hollowstar House, the outdoor lamp sprang on and the door clanged open. Jackie glared down at them. She wasn't smiling.

Chapter Twenty-Seven

His obedient followers stood in the gloom as he circled the desk. He took stock of the damage, pushing papers aside, noting what was missing.

He should have been here. He should have kept his focus on the girl. The tricksy little pest!

He should have destroyed the script when he had the chance. He should have burnt it to a crisp. But he had not! Maybe he was growing sentimental in his old age. He must have caught something from the humans – some weakness of the heart.

He roared, upturning the table and sending it crashing to the floor. His followers did not flinch. He snapped his teeth at them but they were empty. They were no fun any more.

He slumped into a chair.

He still felt tired. This new body felt bony and tight. How he longed to stretch, feel his old strength return again. One more night until he could bathe in the beam of the Hay Moon.

He kicked the mess at his feet. He would have to take more precautions to stop the girl. Surely she could not have worked it out. All was not lost.

He sat back and began to reel off his orders. His followers stood up straighter and marched away to do his new bidding. Such clumsy, tiresome servants but they all had their uses. Some more useful than others.

He must be gone too. It was time to prepare for the Hay Moon.

CHAPTER TWENTY-EIGHT

Kallie didn't think she'd ever felt worse in her life. She, Marlow and Emilia sat together on the sofa in Hollowstar House, all three staring at their feet as Jackie stormed in front of them.

'I never thought that Wildstormers could be capable of such deceitful behaviour.' Kallie could feel Jackie's eyes drilling into her forehead. 'Mr Mildew tells me you broke into his house and smashed an extremely valuable Ming vase!'

Kallie swallowed. She didn't want to point out that actually it had been the Enchanted boy's head that had smashed the vase.

'Now, I don't care for Mr Mildew' – Jackie paused in her pacing of the living room – 'but this is not acceptable. Not least because I have just attended a village meeting at which I promised that soggy-brained old fart that none of my Wildstormers would ever be involved in errant behaviour. Now you've proved Mr

Mildew right! What have you got to say for yourselves?'

All three stayed silent. Kallie had rolled around the idea and decided that if they did show the missing script to Jackie, she'd more than likely give it back to Mr Mildew. They couldn't afford to lose it.

'You three are banned from the play,' said Jackie curtly.

Marlow let out a squeal like a deflated balloon.

Emilia cried: 'Mum! What!?'

And Kallie stared at the floor, shame washing over her.

'Emilia, do not take that tone with me. This was a step too far. It's hard enough with the villagers against us – once they find out what you've done, this could be the end of Wildstorm!' Jackie swallowed hard; Kallie could see this was painful for her. 'I will not permit you to perform tomorrow,' commanded Jackie. 'Your parts will be given to other members of the cast.'

'But Emilia had nothing to do with it,' Kallie protested. 'She was here the whole time.'

'I have no doubt that Emilia was involved in this distasteful plot from the beginning,' said Jackie, pulling herself upright and narrowly missing a beam in the ceiling. 'I come back to find the kitchen wrecked and poor Burn with a bump on his head – the man might have a concussion. His eyes are all out of focus—'

'He's not himself!' Kallie couldn't hold back, and suddenly found herself on her feet. 'He's not – they're not – Mr Mildew – Ellsabet – please—'

Jackie seemed to grow with anger. 'I will not have talk of that made-up, village-nonsense witch's curse in this house!' she boomed.

'You don't understand, she wasn't a witch – it's not Ellsabet – it's someone else!'

'It's no good!' Emilia tugged Kallie's arm.

Kallie remained standing; her face was burning with the injustice of it all. Marlow hadn't said a word. He looked utterly dumbfounded.

'Kallie Tamm, sit down!' Jackie scowled. 'I don't want to hear any more about it. Now go to bed and in the morning, you can make breakfast for those cast members who *will* be performing. But for you three, the show is over.'

Kallie couldn't sleep that night. She knew what missing out on the play would mean to Emilia and Marlow. She was gutted herself, but if they didn't act soon then Merricombe and Wildstorm might be changed for ever. It was clear the Wrathlok was knitting together the wall of hatred and distrust between the villagers and

Wildstormers. And if they didn't stop him, Wildstorm might be no more.

Adrenaline was burning inside her. The Wrathlok – the demon who had caused Ellsabet's death – was sleeping in a stately house a mere ten minutes down the road. A demon who could camouflage as a human really was a perfect disguise. Of course, the Wrathlok would choose Mr Mildew, with his authority and influence in the village. This was all beyond Kallie's worst nightmares.

There was still a nagging feeling in the pit of her stomach: what if she wasn't the new Storyteller? What if she wasn't the one who could defeat him? She didn't have any special powers. She barely had the confidence to share her plays with other people. When she was younger, she used to like sharing her stories in class but then teachers kept complaining about her spelling and handwriting – it was like they couldn't see her story behind the smokescreen of mistakes. And then she'd been diagnosed with dyslexia. How could a great Storyteller be dyslexic? Shouldn't the Storyteller be at ease with words, rather than at odds with them?

She sat up, pulled her bag on to her lap and took out her notebook and the missing script. She looked down at the line she'd written a few days ago.

I may not be a hero, but I am braver than you think.

She could imagine bravery in a story – on a stage – but living it was entirely different. She closed the notebook and turned to the script. She re-read the Storyteller's final speech, muttering the words aloud. She just had to trust that Ellsabet knew what she was doing. She had to trust Ellsabet's words.

Early the next morning, Kallie was woken up by Violet calling outside her tent. She felt like a wrung-out cloth: tired and drained.

She, Emilia and Marlow shuffled around the kitchen, Smudge getting under their feet. In between making beans on toast for the hungry Wildstormers, they filled in Emilia on their night's adventure. Emilia's face glowed when Kallie told her about Arley coming back to himself.

'I wish you could know him – the real him,' Emilia corrected herself dismally.

When the other cast members arrived, many of them thought their new cooks were there as a joke. But soon the details of their punishment started to spread. Most of the cast were shocked and hurt – especially the three chosen to take over their parts, in addition to their own. Ivan was doubling for Marlow; he was pink and terrified as he looked over the script, gulping down his breakfast.

'So the final speech is the spell Ellsabet used on the Wrathlok?' said Emilia, when there was a lull in the breakfast queue. 'Let me have a look at the script again.'

'But I thought you said Ellsabet wasn't a real witch,' said Marlow. 'How can she just do a magic spell?'

'Ellsabet had been learning about the Wrathlok,' said Kallie, handing the script to Emilia. 'She must have found out the right words to stop him.'

'Why didn't you just do the spell at Mr Mildew last night?' said Marlow, mixing the cauldron of baked beans with a grumpy expression.

'Because of the stage directions, silly,' said Emilia. 'It says: "THE STORYTELLER holds her weapon high." We need the weapon.'

'Maybe it's a broomstick,' said Marlow, handing Kallie the wet plates.

'No!' said Kallie, exasperatedly. 'The weapon wouldn't be something like that.'

'OK. What about a sword?' sighed Marlow.

'Ellsabet believed that words were more powerful,' said Kallie, stacking the plates.

There was a terrific splash as Emilia dropped a pan in the sink. 'But Kallie, that's it! Of course!'

'I'm soaking!' Marlow sniffed, soap suds in his perfect hair.

'Words! The weapon! Where's Rose's letter?' Emilia was bright-eyed again.

Kallie hastily dried her hands on her jeans and pulled Rose's letter from her rucksack in the corner.

'Here! Look what Rose says,' said Emilia. She read aloud: '"'Brute force will not stop him,' was Ellsabet's reply" . . . blah blah blah . . . oh yes! "We will defeat him with the quill." And in the speech it says "There is magic in my quill". The weapon *is* the quill!'

Kallie and Emilia beamed at each other.

'The pen is mightier than the sword,' said Kallie. 'I heard that once.'

'Maybe you've got to be holding the quill when you say the spell? Or maybe you've got to poke him in the eye with it! But the quill's important, right?' said Emilia.

Kallie nodded. 'There's just one thing . . .' She fiddled with her hair. 'Why didn't the spell defeat the Wrathlok last time? It made him disappear and it saved the Enchanted, but why didn't it totally work? The villagers were still brainwashed by the Wrathlok and

209

Ellsabet said she knew the Wrathlok would come back.'

'Maybe it needs to be done twice,' said Emilia. 'Maybe two Storytellers need to do it before it works.'

Kallie shrugged, but said nothing. She just hoped Emilia's theory was correct. Something still didn't feel quite right – but Kallie pushed her doubts aside.

'OK,' said Emilia. 'We've got the spell and the quill and the successor of Ellsabet Graveheart,' she said, ticking them off her fingers. 'What more do you need to defeat a demon?'

'Arley said he would be strongest after sunset on the Hay Moon,' said Kallie.

'So we've got until sunset tonight?' said Marlow, sitting on the counter. 'Or those Enchanted will be stuck like that and the villagers will stop Wildstorm! I can't believe I'm not even in it!'

'Yes, that's the *main* tragedy!' scoffed Emilia, rolling her eyes.

'But we don't have very long,' said Marlow. 'And the quill's being used in the play; we can't just take it.'

'Marlow, Marlow.' Emilia shook her head at him. 'Welcome to the way we do things on this adventure.' She grinned. 'Obviously, we're going to steal it. What do you think, Kallie?'

Kallie was fiddling with her rucksack strap. They

were both looking at her, as if waiting for instructions. As if she, Kallie, was somehow in charge. She couldn't share her doubts with her friends; she had to be strong – or at least, try to be strong.

'OK. Once we have the quill, let's go to The Ferns and trap Mr Mildew in his house. Stop him getting to the Hay Moon, and I'll try the speech-spell thing. Entrapping a demon shouldn't be too difficult, right?'

Kallie forced a grin and Emilia and Marlow grinned back, relieved and emboldened.

The plan was agreed in quick whispers as they finished off the washing up. Jackie had a list of jobs that would keep them busy most of the day – helping with the final paint touch-ups on set, sorting out biscuits and squash, making lunch, putting up signs for the audience and hanging up costumes while Dotty went to buy extra pins. They would have to wait until just before the performance began before they had a chance to slip away unnoticed.

It was a difficult waiting game. Sunset was only hours away. Kallie's mind couldn't settle on anything else. Violet kept asking her if she was feeling all right, as Kallie helped her set up the chairs in the auditorium.

By 5 p.m., the pre-show panic had begun. Parents

and friends would be travelling to Merricombe and the performance would start at 6 p.m. that evening. Everyone was frantic with last-minute preparations.

Jackie was standing at the theatre doors, bellowing commands: 'I need the King's Courtiers onstage now – not the Lord's Soldiers – I don't want to see any Lord's Soldiers! Dotty, we need Maria's beard! DOTTY! Where is this young lady's beard!?'

Violet was dealing with one of the Narrators, who had fallen backwards off the stage: 'If we wipe off the blood, the audience won't even notice your missing tooth! Just make it part of your character!'

Their time to sneak away had arrived. Kallie ducked past Violet and hurried up the aisle between the chairs. Everyone was bustling around, half-dressed in velvet capes and muddy jeans, re-reading scripts, their lips moving soundlessly as they practised their lines. Kallie felt a moment of regret that she was not part of it. Their excitement streamed around her as if she was an island.

In Kallie's pocket, she had a black feather they'd found Smudge playing with in the garden. They'd quickly painted it green with the leftover paint from the set, before Ray had noticed. She'd make the exchange and get out of there.

Kallie climbed on to the stage and skirted around Ivan and the King's Courtiers, who were running their lines for the first scene; Kallie shot Ivan a quick thumbs up before slipping backstage. She squeezed through the shouts and clatter to the costume cupboard. It was a small room so stuffed with wigs and shoes and puffy skirts there was hardly space to manoeuvre. Kallie paused in the doorway; Dotty was inside, her back to Kallie, bending over her sewing machine.

'I'm just fetching something for Violet,' said Kallie brightly, spying the green quill on the hanger marked 'Storyteller'.

Dotty didn't respond; maybe she hadn't heard her. Kallie darted to the costume and swapped the feathers. The moment her hand closed over the emerald quill, she felt something leap inside her. She felt braver.

'Um – I'll just take this and go, if that's OK?' said Kallie to Dotty's back.

The costumer said nothing. In fact, she was oddly still. Kallie's breath caught in her throat. She took a step closer. Dotty sat frozen at her sewing machine; her eyes were blank and glassy.

Kallie tripped backwards, almost falling into a box of hats, her heart banging fiercely. Another Enchanted. Kallie backed out of the room and fled. Pushing through the crowds, she ran around the back of the theatre, a stitch in her side.

'He's got Dotty,' Kallie exclaimed, seeing Emilia and Marlow up ahead waiting near the secret door, which had been padlocked shut by Jackie. 'We've got to go now!'

'I've got the rope,' said Emilia. 'Ray had a spare bit for the set.'

'Now don't be annoyed,' began Marlow, 'but I couldn't resist grabbing a sword. Don't look at me like that! It's a bloomin' sword – it'll come in handy! We're talking about defeating a demon here—'

'We will defeat him with the quill!' intoned Emilia. 'That's what Rose said in her letter.'

'We'd better get going,' said Kallie, putting a stop to their squabbling. 'This way—'

But there was someone standing behind them. Seven people. Six Enchanted. Arley, his two friends, the two girls from Fallow Hill and Dotty.

'Not these clowns again!' Marlow gulped.

The Enchanted pounced. Everything happened so fast; two of the boys seized Marlow and threw a cloth bag over his head – Kallie blundered towards him but Dotty grabbed her and was twisting her arms behind her. Emilia was pummelling at the Enchanted girl holding her, kicking and swearing.

'Not so fast!' a voice resounded behind them.

Kallie twisted to see Ivan, wearing Marlow's costume – his golden robe fluttering in the breeze and the plastic crown perched on his head – framed by the sun behind him. His sword in hand, Ivan charged at the Enchanted – one of them stuck out his leg and Ivan fell as if in slow motion with a great cry of 'Oooooohh nooo!'

'Don't hurt him!' Kallie shouted, as two of the Enchanted children surrounded Ivan. 'Don't—'

But a bag was pulled roughly over her head and everything went black.

CHAPTER TWENTY-NINE

Kallie opened her eyes. The first thing she noticed was the light – a fiery orange flicker somewhere far above her.

She turned her head, her neck stiff. They were in a concrete room, empty but for a small window set high in the wall. The ebbing sun glinted through the glass. Marlow was splayed on the ground beside her and Emilia was on her other side, her head on her knees. Over in a corner, Ivan sat huddled against the wall, still wearing the King's costume.

'Em? Emilia?' Kallie found her voice. 'Marlow?'

She stood up, her head buzzing.

'Where are we?' Ivan murmured, as Kallie helped him to his feet.

'We're sorry, we didn't mean to drag you into this,' Kallie said, 'but there's no time to explain.'

'We're at The Ferns,' said Marlow, craning his neck to see out of the window. 'I can see the driveway and the golf cart. At least we're in the right place.'

'We're trapped in the cellar!' croaked Emilia, rubbing her head.

Marlow strode to the door and gave it an experimental push. It didn't move.

'It's locked,' he said unhelpfully. He squinted through the keyhole. 'There are three of them outside. Dotty's not there; she must have gone back to the theatre. It's just the three boys. Arley's there. They've got mine and Ivan's swords and the rope and the quill.'

'It's almost sunset,' said Emilia, clambering to her feet. 'He must know we're trying to stop him. The Hay Moon will be out soon! Kallie, what now?'

'Hay what?' Ivan interjected but they ignored him.

'He wants to keep us here until after sunset,' said Kallie, her mouth dry. 'Until it's all over and he's all-powerful.'

'So what's the plan, Kallie?' said Marlow, echoing Emilia.

Kallie looked between them and saw the hope in their eyes. They really thought she could help them. They really thought she had a clue. Kallie felt a crushing wave of guilt.

'I . . . I don't know what to do,' she said at last. 'I – I don't know how I can help. I don't have any special powers. Maybe I'm not . . . not what Ellsabet hoped for in a successor.'

She couldn't look at them. Panic was preventing her from thinking. She felt sick and empty. This was it. She should never have assumed that she could be a hero.

'Kallie, listen to me!' Emilia folded her arms and she sounded so much like Jackie that Kallie looked up in surprise. 'Yes, things seem pretty doom and gloom right now but I once read a play that said that true heroes aren't always the strongest or the most powerful, but they're the ones who never give up.'

Kallie stared at her, shocked.

'It's from *The Unlikely Hero*,' said Emilia gently, 'the play you wrote for the Wildstorm Playwriting Competition. Don't tell me you've forgotten it already?! It really stuck with me. Your story. It's true. We're not giving up.'

Kallie felt like she'd been zapped with an electric charge. She'd never realised that her stories could mean something to other people. But stories were powerful – for evil and for good. And the thought had given Kallie an idea.

'There might be something,' she said, a new energy humming inside her.

She hurried over to the door and put her eye to the keyhole. Outside, she saw a stone corridor with a bench where the swords, the rope and the quill lay. The Enchanted stood beside it, docile as sleeping horses. Arley stood closest to the door, a key dangling from his belt. Her plan might just work. She straightened up and turned to the others.

'I'm going to try talking to Arley,' she said and Emilia's face lit up. 'It worked before – I managed to wake him up last time so maybe it'll work again.'

'What's wrong with them?' piped up Ivan.

'They're being mind-controlled by a demon called the Wrathlok,' said Emilia quickly.

'Wrath . . . who?'

'But what about the other ones?' Marlow pointed out. 'They'll stop us. And Arley'll stop us if he goes all Enchanted again.'

'We'll have to be ready,' agreed Kallie.

'Wait! I've got an idea,' said Marlow. 'You handle Arley and I've got a way we can take care of the others.'

Emilia, Marlow and Ivan stationed themselves around the door and Kallie bent down to the keyhole and took a deep breath.

'Arley?' No response. The Enchanted boy's face

remained unmoving. 'Arley, I know you're inside – so listen as hard as you can. You're stronger than you think. I need you to remember – you need to find yourself again.'

Kallie went on, sensing the stares of the others behind her. She told Arley a story about himself and Emilia at Wildstorm, their friendship and loyalty, and how disaster struck – a fire had started in the theatre and Emilia was trapped inside but Arley had run back through the smoke, unlocked the door and pulled her to safety. Even though it wasn't a true story, Kallie had a feeling it was the story Arley needed. A story of courage and hope. As she spoke, Kallie remembered how Ellsabet had told stories to the village kids and how those stories had fed their hearts and minds.

Kallie was almost at the end of her tale when she saw Arley blink. He frowned dazedly, as if emerging from a deep sleep.

'Emilia?' he muttered, looking around him, disorientated.

'We're in the cellar!' Emilia cried. 'Use the key! You've got it!'

Arley staggered towards the locked door, his movements stiff and awkward; he fitted the key in the lock. Kallie grinned back at the others; Emilia was beaming, Marlow was tensed and Ivan looked stunned.

'Emilia! Remember the plan,' hissed Marlow through gritted teeth.

The door swung open and Marlow and Kallie dived past Arley towards the two still-Enchanted boys, stretching the fabric belt from the King's costume between them. The belt caught the boys in the stomach before they could react and brought them crashing to the floor.

'Quick – Ivan, get the rope!' roared Marlow and Ivan scooped it up from the bench and threw it to him.

Kallie, Marlow and Ivan wrapped the rope around the Enchanted boys and tied it to the bench. The boys struggled unsuccessfully against the knots.

'Let's get out of here!' cried Kallie, snatching up the quill as Marlow grabbed the swords. 'We don't have much time.'

She looked back at Emilia, who had thrown her arms around Arley and was whooping with excitement. Marlow and Kallie darted towards her but before they reached her, Arley's eyes had misted over and his arms tensed around Emilia – he started dragging her back into the cellar.

'No!'

Marlow and Kallie seized Emilia, pulling her out of Arley's grip.

'Run!' Kallie yelled, grabbing Ivan's wrist in her free hand; they hurtled down the corridor and up the stone steps at the end. Arley pursued them, all sense of himself forgotten.

They burst through a door at the top of the stairs and slammed it shut behind them, just in time.

'Get that table!' Marlow called.

Ivan dragged it across the floor and they pressed it against the door, just as Arley hit the other side with an almighty force. The door held.

'I told you to stick to the plan!' Marlow squawked at Emilia, who looked white and shaken.

'It doesn't matter. Come on! It might not hold him for long!' cried Kallie, racing along another corridor and into the entrance hall.

The Ferns was eerily silent; even the thumps from the basement were muffled. Mr Mildew – the Wrathlok – was nowhere to be seen.

'He's gone,' said Kallie, wrenching open the front doors. '"*On the night of the Hay Moon, the demon heads for high ground to tell his tale to the moon*",' she repeated from Rose's letter. 'Fallow Hill! The highest point in Merricombe – that's where he's gone.'

The sun was easing down the horizon, shooting dark orange shapes across the lawn. The Hay Moon was visible now like a ghost in the sky. Kallie started down the steps but a shout called her back:

'Um . . . I need some help here!' Ivan was half holding Emilia; she had slumped to the floor.

Kallie and Marlow rushed over. Emilia was pale and clammy, her eyes darting fitfully.

'Kallie,' Emilia croaked, 'my head . . .'

Kallie looked down; there was a dark smudge on Emilia's wrist. A black moon tattooed on her skin. Before Kallie could say anything, her friend's eyes clouded over. Emilia stiffened and then stood up jerkily, turning to face towards the setting sun.

'No! Emilia! No!' Kallie seized her friend's arm. 'He can't—'

There were tears in Kallie's eyes now. She couldn't let this happen.

'We've got to go!' Marlow's hair was standing on end, his eyes wild. 'It's almost sunset and we need to get to Fallow Hill in the next twenty minutes! *Now* would be a good time for a broomstick. We need – wait! I've got another idea. We'll take the cart!'

He pointed to the golf cart in the middle of the lawn.

'Kallie! Come on!' Marlow grabbed her sleeve.

'Leave Emilia! We don't know what she'll do! She could be dangerous.'

'I'm not leaving her,' said Kallie, holding Emilia's arm as if it was a lifebelt. 'She's still in there, I know she is.'

Kallie looked out at the approaching sunset. The demon had just made a fatal mistake – there was no way Kallie was going to stop now. She was still terrified, but that didn't matter any more, because there was nothing she wouldn't do to save her friend.

CHAPTER THIRTY

The low sun stained the trees red, the branches streaked with crimson, leaves like scarlet and golden flames. It looked like the whole wood was on fire.

The little golf cart strained up the hill, Marlow at the wheel, Ivan beside him, and Emilia and Kallie in the back seat. Emilia was staring straight ahead, the light dimmed behind her eyes. Kallie was muttering to her – every story, every fun memory they'd shared in the last week, Kallie described it to her friend.

'And then Smudge stole those biscuits and sneezed when he ate the ginger ones.'

'Smudge . . .' Emilia mumbled but her voice was distant.

You can't keep him out for much longer, said a voice in Kallie's head. *You're not as strong as Ellsabet.* She struggled to push it away – there wasn't time to doubt herself.

The golf cart jolted violently, almost toppling

sideways, and Kallie had to grab hold of Emilia to stop her falling. The little cart was not built for uphill climbs.

'We're almost there!' cried Marlow. 'Oh no! Look!'

Kallie twisted around and she saw figures walking up Fallow Hill between the trees. More village children, including Arley and the others from The Ferns. It hadn't taken them long to escape the cellar. It was a whole army of Enchanted.

'They're all going to him.' Kallie swallowed.

'So what's the plan?' Marlow cried over the groaning engine.

'I've got to do the spell before sunset,' Kallie called back. 'I just hope we get there in time.'

'W-what if those weird people hurt us?' squeaked Ivan; he was still wearing his over-large costume.

'We'll give them a battering,' said Marlow, gripping his sword; he'd stuck both of them into the place where the golf clubs usually went.

'No!' pleaded Kallie. 'Don't hurt them. They don't know what they're doing.'

'Then how are we supposed to stop them?' Marlow looked from Kallie to Ivan. 'Wait a moment – I'm about to be a genius! The King's robe!'

'This isn't the time for a costume change!' said Kallie wildly.

'I'm not going to wear it; I need what's in the pockets,' replied Marlow and he leant over to Ivan and extracted a cylinder from his costume.

'A smoke flare,' cried Kallie. 'How did you know they were there?'

'I – whoever's playing the King – was supposed to bring two flares onstage,' said Marlow quickly. 'I know it's not much but just hear me out . . .'

The golf cart gave up before they reached the hilltop, its wheels spinning hopelessly on the slope. They left it leaning against a tree, whining sadly. The four of them crept forward on foot. Emilia's eyes were clouding over; she seemed to be sinking deeper into the enchantment. Kallie held tight to her arm. She fought to keep her fear at bay – she couldn't lose hope now; she had to keep going.

As they reached the edge of the trees, a strange sight dazzled them. The hilltop was alive with lights. Flaming sticks were stuck into the ground, like giant matches, their flames curling in the wind. The Enchanted had formed a wide circle around the blackthorn stump. And there, in the centre of it all, was Mr Mildew.

Emilia's struggles redoubled and Kallie could hardly hold her back.

'We've got to stick to the plan,' said Marlow. 'The smoke flare will only last twenty seconds. Emilia will be all right but we need you, Kallie.'

'OK.'

Kallie's throat was sore as she let go of Emilia's arm and watched her walk away and take her place in the circle bedside Arley. Marlow was right: stick to the plan. She gripped Ellsabet's quill. Every instinct inside Kallie was telling her to run – to hide – but she took a shuddering breath and began to walk up the hill, Marlow and Ivan behind her.

'Demon! We've come to stop you!' Kallie called, the smoke from the flaming sticks stinging her throat.

Mr Mildew turned slowly, leaning on his cane.

'Welcome, Storyteller.' He spoke in a strange sing-song voice.

'I – I am the successor of Ellsabet Graveheart, the new Storyteller,' Kallie cried, feeling every Enchanted eye in the clearing rotating to scrutinise her. 'I – I have a spell written by Ellsabet Graveheart, which will destroy you.'

Before Mr Mildew could respond, Kallie raised Ellsabet's quill and yelled: 'Now!'

There was a great bang as Marlow leapt forward, a smoke flare in his hand. Red smoke mushroomed into the air and Kallie charged forward, head low, aiming for Mr Mildew. The quill in one hand and the script in the other, she started reciting Ellsabet's speech, but she could hardly see Mr Mildew through the coloured fog. The Enchanted were blundering into each other – a hand came out of nowhere, a moon tattoo on its wrist, and seized Kallie's hair.

'Nooo!!' Marlow leapt into view and elbowed the boy out of the way.

Kallie kept on running.

'*You may choose the face you wear and a voice to match, Dress up in human skin to suit the plots you hatch,*' she recited. '*Ancient, restless spirit, you will not win again—*'

And suddenly she reached him, the hunched figure by the tree stump. Driven by her momentum, Kallie bowled into Mr Mildew and they both fell hard on the ground; Mr Mildew's cane flew from his hand.

'*There is magic in my voice, magic in my quill; With these words I conquer and overturn your will!*'

Unsure what to do next, Kallie screwed up her eyes and stuck the quill into one of Mr Mildew's flailing arms – but something was wrong. The smoke was clearing; Mr Mildew was shuffling away from her, torn and rumpled, his eyes unfocused. And then Kallie saw the mark on his wrist – the full moon.

'But – but you're enchanted?'

Kallie scrabbled to her feet and Mr Mildew continued to stare at her. Horror struck Kallie's heart. This man was no demon.

'Did you really think I'd use a shrivelled, old body like that?' came a voice behind her – Kallie spun around.

Walking through the simmering smoke towards her, dragging Marlow by the collar, was Ivan.

CHAPTER THIRTY-ONE

The Wrathlok – the one who could wear many faces and speak in many voices – stalked towards Kallie. The fading light was behind Ivan, bathing him in a fiery glow. Only it wasn't Ivan behind that terrible smile. As he stepped closer, he seemed to grow taller, Ivan's round face distorted with cruelty. The eyes were worst of all. Hollow tunnels of darkness with pupils like flickering fire.

Kallie couldn't run. She dropped to her knees, the script slipping from her fingers, as the demon loomed above her. He threw Marlow aside and Marlow scrambled behind Kallie. The Wrathlok, the Ivan-demon, bent down and plucked the quill from Mr Mildew's limp arm. The Enchanted man didn't even flinch; he just stared ahead.

'Alas, your plan has failed.' Ivan's familiar voice crackled like autumn leaves. 'You've brought your friends into danger and all is lost.'

He dropped the quill on the ground and his small teeth curved in a smile. He shook the golden robe from his shoulders and Kallie watched it fall in the dirt: a useless costume from a make-believe play, which now seemed a lifetime away.

'What? No words from Ellsabet's successor?' He sniffed. 'I thought you were full of words – so full of stories – Kallie Tamm.'

The Wrathlok cackled. Above him, the moon was like a great white eye in the sky. The sunlight was draining away. Night was closing in.

'You – you can't!' Kallie croaked, but it seemed such a foolish thing to say.

'Oh yes I can! So melodramatic.' He gave her a withering look. 'It is time for the curtain to fall on your little adventure.'

Suddenly, he lunged forward and seized her wrist, squeezing his fingers into the spot where the Enchanted wore their tattoos. And Kallie felt him pressing into her mind – his voice echoing in every chamber of her head. It vibrated through her thoughts, her dreams and her memories . . .

'*Emilia was never your friend,*' the voice rumbled inside her head, '*she never liked you. You cheated at the playwriting competition, don't you remember?*

You've never won anything. You're weak and shy. Whoever heard of a dyslexic playwright? You could never be Ellsabet's successor.'

Images were speeding in front of Kallie's eyes: Jackie announcing the Wildstorm play, Emilia picking up Smudge, her mum hugging her goodbye. These images vanished into darkness and Kallie felt a terrible emptiness welling up inside her.

'STOP!' With a huge effort, Kallie forced her mind to remember – Ellsabet, Rose, Emilia, Marlow; she had to fight for them. She pushed against the demon's voice and the darkness evaporated.

She found herself lying on the ground, panting.

'A bold move.' The Wrathlok peered down at her. 'Your mind is strong. I saw that in the cellar. I was impressed with your trick on that boy – that's why I let you do it. But soon your pathetic little imagination will be lost for ever. I will make you empty, just like them.'

Kallie looked up at the Enchanted, standing in their silent circle, and her throat tightened with terror. Emilia stood amongst them, her face blank and expressionless. But something had changed. Kallie could sense the emptiness inside them now; the terrible darkness that clouded their minds seemed to pulse in the air around them. She could hear something, a faint whispering. The Enchanted were calling to her. She could hear their voices in her head. Underneath the demon's magic, they were still there, begging her for help.

The Wrathlok turned his face to the night sky.

'Before the nastiness begins, I owe you thanks,' he purred. 'I would never have awoken if you had not come to Merricombe. I felt the presence of a Storyteller in my slumbers and I rose once more. And it feels oh so good to be back. Yet now it is time for the final act. Prepare my stage!'

The Enchanted instantly started to move around the clearing, lighting more sticks and pushing them into the ground around the blackthorn stump. Some of them had buckets of white paint and began to draw symbols on the dry grass. Kallie fought back waves of panic. She looked across to Marlow, bruised and beaten; he looked desperately at Kallie. But what could she do? She was just as scared as him.

'Ellsabet knew you'd return,' Kallie croaked and the demon's eyes spun back to her. 'She told me how to defeat you. The script—'

'Has failed.' The Wrathlok smiled nastily. 'Ellsabet may have spun her little spell on me four hundred years ago – she may have stopped me reaching the

Hay Moon – but she never really defeated me and nor can you. Soon I shall return to my true form' – he ran his hands over his small, human arms – 'more powerful than ever. Then I shall go down to the theatre and make the villagers burn it to the ground. You will be powerless to stop me.'

Behind him, the Enchanted were performing their tasks with quick precision – soon they would have covered the grass in white symbols and the demon's moon ceremony would begin. Kallie could still feel the Enchanted murmuring faintly, their panic and fear beating in her own heart.

'These people never did anything to hurt you,' Kallie blurted out. 'It's not fair.'

The demon grinned. His face was less human now, dark hollows etched into the cheeks.

'Where's the fun in being fair?' he leered. 'These last few days have been the most excitement I've had in four hundred years. I was a little groggy when I awoke – I could barely remember why I had been asleep – but soon my old abilities returned to me.'

'So you used Arley and his friends to find out what was going on – you used them to spy on Wildstorm?' said Kallie, with half an eye on the Enchanted's progress. 'They found out about Ellsabet's play. But you wanted to know more so you sent them to get the key to the theatre. You were so obsessed with Ellsabet, that's why the Enchanted were always chanting her name.'

The demon gave a slow clap, the sound echoing dully.

'Very clever. It took me a while to find answers – to find my new opponent. It was during that mischief on the hilltop when I first saw you. I recognised you at once. You have the same foolish bravery of Ellsabet. So I decided to keep a closer eye on you.'

'You took Ivan,' gulped Kallie. 'You took him over as your disguise that night.'

'Believe me, it's not as comfortable as it might look,' said the demon, examining Ivan's fingernails, 'especially if you get one the wrong size – the itching is unbearable!'

'Where's Ivan now?' Marlow squeaked, still cowering behind Kallie.

'He's still in here, somewhere inside.' The Wrathlok sniggered. 'But soon I will have the strength to leave his flimsy human body. Ivan will be an empty shell.'

The last rays of sunset were crawling across the clearing as the Enchanted continued to paint on the grass. Kallie was hoping a plan would pop into her head, hoping Marlow would think of something as she played for time.

'So you knew I was a Wildstormer and you started turning the village against us. You must have got one of your Enchanted to send Mr Mildew that message about Ellsabet's play,' she said. 'You needed him to start stirring up the old rumours about Ellsabet the Witch.'

He laughed softly and Kallie felt the hairs on her arms stand on end.

'It only takes a whisper for a story to take hold,' he hissed. 'That is the terrible power of stories, Kallie, their power for spreading fear and hatred.'

'Not all stories.'

'The ones that stick,' leered the demon. 'We can make them feel and think however we want. You can control them, Kallie, as I do. After all, I learnt my storytelling from humans. I watched the humans spreading lies and taunts – it looked like fun so I gave it a whirl and it turns out I'm a natural!'

'Ellsabet wanted to use stories for good,' countered Kallie; she felt cold. 'Ellsabet wanted to help people.'

She stared up at him. Something had awoken in the back of her mind. An idea was nagging at her but she couldn't quite grasp it.

'You got the Enchanted to write that message on the

door and steal the costumes,' muttered Kallie, turning it all over in her mind. 'And when you were strong enough you enchanted Mr Mildew . . . you must have got him that afternoon when we returned the costumes. I thought he seemed a bit odd. He went all quiet and when Jackie told him to leave, he just walked off without a word.'

'As much as I'm enjoying your review of my performance,' the Wrathlok sneered, 'I really do have things to attend to.'

Behind him, the painted symbols were almost complete and Kallie recognised them as huge versions of the Enchanted's tattoos: from the waxing crescent to the full orb, the stages of the moon were painted on the grass around the blackthorn stump. The sight reminded Kallie of something.

'You tried to enchant Emilia in the theatre,' said Kallie thoughtfully, 'during the fencing – but you couldn't because of the witch's marks! Of course, Ellsabet was learning about you; she must have etched those marks into the theatre and Hollowstar House for extra protection. She told Rose to stay in the house when they knew you were back and she locked John and his father in the theatre when they became enchanted. The theatre's protected by the witch's marks. You must have enchanted Dotty when she went out for extra pins and Burn when he wasn't in the kitchen.'

'Those charms are silly penny-stall tricks.' He sniffed. 'They will not stop me once I am all-powerful.'

'The Enchanted stole those books on lucky charms from the Historical Society,' Kallie murmured, her mind whirring. 'You didn't want anyone learning how to protect themselves . . . Then you found the missing script at The Ferns – Mr Mildew must have taken it out before he was enchanted – and you got him to keep it safe, didn't you?' said Kallie triumphantly. 'Well, he didn't do a very good job.'

'As you have learnt tonight, the script will not help you,' he snorted. 'You've made the same foolish mistake as Ellsabet. You did a very pretty performance of her speech just now and nothing happened.'

'But why target the Wildstorm play?' Kallie said suddenly. 'Why not turn everyone against me, like you did with Ellsabet? I'm the successor. Why not just punish me? Why attack Wildstorm and the theatre?'

'I do not need a reason to cause mischief!' cried the demon. 'Mayhem sustains me. Fear feeds me.' But Kallie thought she saw a shiver of unease in his eyes.

The demon was lying to her.

'Enough chatter,' he growled. 'The Hay Moon is ready.'

He turned his back on Kallie and the Enchanted glided away to re-form the circle, their task complete. The moon now shone bright and bold. All that remained of the sunset was a trickle of golden light on the horizon. Time was up.

Kallie remained still, everything that had been said churning inside her. Whatever the demon said, Kallie was sure he was somehow afraid of the theatre and the missing script. Kallie forced herself to think!

Why did the Wrathlok want to stop Wildstorm doing the play? And why hadn't Ellsabet been able to defeat him before? Ellsabet had done the spell but something had been missing. What?

But then the truth finally blazed through Kallie. She gasped. Ellsabet had been missing an audience.

On the night she'd tried to defeat the demon, Ellsabet had wanted to perform the play but no one had come. That was it! In order to unleash the full magic, they needed to perform the whole play to an audience and they needed to do it in the theatre. That's why Ellsabet had built it! And Kallie remembered Ellsabet's words from the letter: *'A theatre is the most magical place,'* she told me, *'a place where people share stories and dream as one . . .'*

Kallie glanced towards the Wrathlok as he climbed on to the blackthorn tree stump. He lifted his face to the moon and began to mutter, hoarse and low, and to her horror she saw his skin start to glow. The Enchanted were forming a tighter circle around the stump and began to chant, holding up candles to the night sky. Kallie could still feel the Enchanted's voices calling to her but they were growing fainter and fainter.

'Marlow,' she whispered. Marlow turned terrified eyes towards her. 'We need to get back to the theatre. I was wrong – it's not just the final speech that is powerful, it's the whole play – and the theatre. Ellsabet wanted us to perform *The King's Downfall* in the theatre – a proper performance to help the play work its magic.'

Hope glimmered in Marlow's face.

'Wildstorm are doing the play right now,' Marlow murmured. 'So we'll be saved!'

'No – they're missing the final speech,' said Kallie, 'and I think I need to perform it – I'm the Storyteller. We've got to get back!'

'The last smoke flare,' croaked Marlow. 'It's still in the robe.'

They both looked at the golden robe, which lay in

the mud an arm's length away. A little beyond it lay the green quill and the script – she'd need them too. Kallie made a tentative movement forward but the Wrathlok had turned his attention on her again.

'Now watch, little Storyteller,' he growled, 'as I return to full strength. Watch and despair.'

The Wrathlok was suddenly illuminated in a beam of moonlight. All thoughts of the plan vanished as Kallie watched, petrified. Ivan's small form was growing, the arms rolling out with muscles and Ivan's features sinking into a gaunt face. The Wrathlok flexed his hands and they seemed to double in size. Fear was like a knife in her side, but Kallie had to act now.

'Arley! Emilia!' Kallie shouted desperately. 'All of you! You're still inside – I can feel it. It's not too late!' She felt a murmur ripple across the clearing and she willed them to understand. 'You're strong. Each of you – I know I don't know you all but I know you've got friends and family – and memories and dreams of your own. Together we can push him out of your minds.'

THUD – Arley had dropped his candle and was blinking at Kallie. The chanting died.

The demon turned with a snarl and Kallie leapt for the robe. She pulled the smoke flare from its pocket and yanked the string, pointing it directly into the Wrathlok's face. The flare exploded like a gunshot – billowing purple smoke obscured the demon. The beam of moonlight vanished.

'Marlow!' Kallie yelled. 'Get Emilia! Get back to the theatre—'

The Wrathlok burst from the smoke. Nothing of Ivan remained. The demon's skin was cracked like the bark of a tree, his feet and hands clawed like thorns, glittering fangs clenched in a grin.

He seized one of the burning sticks and lunged at Kallie – she rolled out of the way just in time. Pandemonium had broken out on Fallow Hill. Some of the Enchanted had come back to themselves and were hurling candles and rocks at the Wrathlok, Arley amongst them, but others were still under his power and were fighting back. The demon stabbed down at Kallie with the flaming stick and she scrambled out of reach.

'Kallie! The sword!' Marlow yelled as he threw the prop sword into the air and it stuck into the ground near Kallie's foot.

Kallie seized it and brought it upwards with all her strength. The sword clashed with the Wrathlok's weapon and she held him off, her arms trembling. He swiped at her with the flaming stick but she deflected it again. She fought back as hard as she could, blocking and dodging and defending – but the demon was too powerful. He caught Kallie's sword in his free hand and tore it from her grip. He kicked out and she was thrown off her feet and landed in the dust. The Wrathlok roared, swelling with triumph. Behind him, Kallie could see Marlow dragging Emilia down the hill towards the golf cart.

'You cannot stop me now. I am the Wrathlok!' he bellowed, flinging the sword aside. 'I am the Great Storyteller bringing terror and hopelessness to all humans.'

The demon opened his arms wide and his Enchanted army froze behind him, every face suddenly empty, awaiting his orders.

Fear was clogging Kallie's insides. She spotted the quill and the script half-submerged in the dirt and the sight of them filled her with renewed bravery – Ellsabet believed she could do this. Before the Wrathlok could move, Kallie threw herself forward and grabbed both quill and script. Clutching them to her chest, she began to roll down the hill, the world spinning as she fell faster and faster down the slope towards the wood.

CHAPTER THIRTY-TWO

Kallie smashed into a tree and gasped, all the strength knocked out of her. The world was slowly coming back into focus, and with it fresh pain and fear: the play . . . the theatre . . . they had to get back!

'Kallie! Over here!' Marlow was screaming from the golf cart. Emilia sat beside him but she was desperate to return to the hilltop, her eyes empty again.

Marlow had already started the engine and Kallie ran to catch up, her head still spinning – she jumped on to the back and it picked up speed. The Wrathlok was shrieking on the hilltop and suddenly the ground began to shake.

'Oh no! They're coming!' cried Marlow.

The Enchanted were marching behind them, smashing through the undergrowth, gaining on them.

'How do you know this is going to work?' screamed Marlow, desperately trying to control the golf cart as it plunged downhill.

'I don't!' Kallie yelled back. 'But Ellsabet built the theatre for a reason! Rose said the play was the answer. Doing that speech on the stage is our last hope!'

'But he's got all – all big – what if it's too late?'

'We can't give up now,' Kallie shouted but the same terrible thought had occurred to her.

Could Ellsabet's play really defeat the Wrathlok at full strength? Kallie pushed her fears aside. They had the quill, the play, the theatre and, well . . . herself, the Storyteller. They just needed to get to the theatre before the play finished or the Enchanted caught them.

The golf cart jerked and Kallie screamed – Emilia's hand had shot out and seized the steering wheel.

'Get her off!' shouted Marlow as the golf cart weaved dangerously, nearly hitting a tree.

Kallie grabbed Emilia's arms.

'Em! Remember who you are,' Kallie cried. 'Remember Smudge! Your mum – and Violet. Hollowstar House! Pepperoni pizza!' she shouted wildly.

Emilia stopped struggling, blinking thoughtfully.

'Pepperoni pizza? Really? That worked?' yelled Marlow over the wind.

The golf cart flew over roots and shrubs. Branches snatched at Kallie's hair, nettles stung her arms; it was as if the whole wood was trying to hold them back.

Then they burst from the trees out into the open meadow beyond the campsite.

'Get ready to jump!' cried Marlow.

They both seized Emilia and leapt from the golf cart, which thundered into the hedge. Footsteps pounded behind them, and another sound rumbled through the wood. The demon was chasing them.

They ran through the campsite, jumping over guy-ropes, dodging the bunting and bouncing off tents. Emilia was trying to pull away from Marlow, her blank face turned to the horror behind them, but Kallie didn't look back. She seized Emilia's other arm and they dragged her onwards.

They rocketed past Hollowstar House and Kallie heard shouts up ahead – something was wrong. They hurtled down the track to the theatre and saw their path blocked by a mass of people. Villagers were brandishing painted signs and angry fists; some were swinging mallets and one even carried a burning stick. Kallie, Marlow and Emilia blundered into the crowd, shoving people aside.

'You've got to get inside the theatre!' Kallie shouted. 'You'll be safer inside!' But her voice barely rose above the babble of hatred radiating from the villagers.

'Burn the theatre down!' screamed one man.

'Stop the witch's curse!' cried an old woman, waving a tartan slipper.

Amidst the swarm, Kallie saw Jackie – her face white with fury – bellowing at Mr Dixson from the Marmalade Café; his usually kindly face was twisted with loathing. Kallie's head swam with panic – it was like a nightmare – she could feel the air hot with fear and the Wrathlok's hateful stories blackening every mind. The seething crowd shunted her this way and that – it was as if she had stepped back in time, for Kallie was certain that this screaming mob was identical to the one that had dragged the innocent Ellsabet to be burnt as a witch, four hundred years ago.

'Please listen to me!' Kallie yelled; she could sense the Enchanted on the track behind them and the demon growing ever closer. 'You've got to get inside the theatre! You're all in danger!'

The theatre doors flew open and the villagers surged over the threshold. Kallie didn't know if the crowd had heard her or not, but it didn't matter. Still holding tight to Emilia's wrist, she and Marlow herded people inside.

'There's a demon coming, you idiots!' Marlow was screaming.

As the last villager stumbled inside, Kallie turned to close the theatre doors but Emilia was suddenly jerked backwards. A black rope had caught Emilia's ankle and she was being pulled away from them.

Kallie turned. The Wrathlok was surging towards them, tugging at the rope holding Emilia; only it wasn't a rope but tendrils of black ivy, writhing like snakes. The trees seemed to have come to life around him; they stretched and creaked, reaching for Kallie and Marlow. They both clung to Emilia but she was slipping away. The Enchanted were skirting around the demon, lumbering towards them.

'Argh!'

A black dot was dancing under the demon's feet and he swatted at it, like a fly, spitting fury. It was Smudge, the little cat leaping and yowling. It was enough of a distraction. With a great effort, Kallie and Marlow dragged Emilia free and barrelled into the theatre.

'Smudge!' Kallie cried.

The cat darted easily between the trees' walloping branches and flew through the open doors. Marlow slammed them shut. They fumbled with the padlock – the door boomed as the demon hit it, shaking like a drum, but it held.

'What on earth is going on?' Jackie demanded. 'Emilia? What's wrong with her?'

The audience peered back at them, a few standing

249

up to get a better view of the unexpected crowd. The villagers were still muttering darkly, anxious eyes flitting this way and that. On the stage, the cast were just finishing the final battle scene, swords flashing, but no one in the audience was paying them any attention any more.

Dodging Jackie, Kallie charged down the aisle towards the stage. She could hear the Wrathlok moving outside the theatre, the trees hammering at the curtained windows, and the beams began to shake as if in a storm. A force hit the walls with an almighty crash – people started to yell.

'Stop her!' the Wrathlok's voice thundered.

Dust was falling from the ceiling and Kallie was almost at the stage but Burn had emerged from nowhere, his Enchanted eyes vacant as his hand seized Kallie's throat.

'Get away from her!' Marlow roared, charging into the old cook and knocking him off balance.

Kallie leapt on to the stage, scattering the cast. The demon gave a roar of frustration from outside the walls.

'Stop the girl! Stop the girl!'

Kallie spun to face the auditorium, holding Ellsabet's quill aloft and pulling the speech from her pocket. She began to read, stuttering over the lines, but she could feel every word fizzing inside her. Her voice rose above the echoing shrieks from the audience.

'You may choose the face you wear and a voice to match,

Dress up in human skin to suit the plots you hatch,

But I know who you are: a demon amongst men.

Ancient, restless spirit, you will not win again!

There is magic in my voice, magic in my quill;

With these words I conquer and overturn your will.'

The doors exploded and the demon blasted into the theatre; splintered wood showered the audience. Kallie coughed and choked, squinting through the falling dust, as the Wrathlok took a step forward. Behind him came his Enchanted army.

'Oh dear, nothing happened.' He grinned. 'Now I will deal with the Storyteller of Merricombe once and for all.'

Kallie didn't understand. How could Ellsabet have let her down like this? The Wildstormers had performed the play, she'd done the speech in the theatre, so why hadn't it worked? She'd followed Ellsabet's directions. Hadn't she? Kallie stared down at the page in her hand and beneath the speech she saw the stage directions:

So THE STORYTELLER speaks, undoing THE KING's power with her words.

Finally she understood. She had to use her *own* words.

The Wrathlok began to pace down the aisle, the audience shrinking away from him.

'I may not be a hero, but I am braver than you think.' Kallie's voice rose, thin but determined. 'I'm brave because of Ellsabet – because Rose kept her story safe, for me. Ellsabet lost her family, she lost everything when you came to her village and turned everyone against her father – but she kept on finding ways to fight you. Even when it seemed impossible, she never gave up. Not all stories spread hatred. Stories can give us hope; they can make us happy, comfort us when we're scared or alone. Stories can make us brave. That's what Ellsabet's story did for me.'

The demon was growing closer, a sickening grin on

his face. Kallie went on, ignoring the tears in her throat and her shaking legs.

'This theatre was built to share stories – to bring people together and make us stronger,' Kallie shouted. 'That's what Wildstorm is all about – we all work together to make something we believe in – a play to share with others. I know I'm just a girl who never wanted to be a hero and you're a mighty demon but I'm going to carry on fighting because that's what Ellsabet would do – your stories cannot frighten me. You cannot take my mind. So be gone from this place!'

The words echoed in Kallie's ears, spiralling up to the ceiling – only it wasn't an echo, it was the sound of many voices shouting together. The Wildstormers around her were caught up in a frenzy, everyone shouting the same words – Kallie's words:

'Be gone from this place!'

Kallie heard Emilia and Jackie shouting together: 'Be gone from this place!'

The audience were yelling too – Kallie caught sight of Arley and his friends adding their voices to the throng. And above them, the witch's marks began to glow like stars. The quill in Kallie's hand started to quiver. She let it go and it hovered unsupported in the air – then it began to write, twirling and looping. It was writing Kallie's words, in her own messy handwriting, the golden letters hanging in mid-air. Kallie gasped as the words shot towards the demon, burning into his skin, he clawing at them, trying to rub them off. His eyes met Kallie's and they burnt with shock and fury.

'I'm sorry,' Kallie whispered, her friends' shouts swelling around her, 'but this is where your story ends.'

He let out a terrible howl – like smoke screaming through a chimney – and the demon burst into ash. Grey flakes showered the audience, covering the stage in dirt and dust. The cloud cleared to reveal Ivan, coughing and spluttering. The demon, the Wrathlok, was gone.

Kallie brushed ash out of her face, her chest still heaving. At the back of the theatre, the Enchanted were looking dazedly around. Burn was disentangling himself from a red-faced Marlow.

Then a slow rhythmic noise started; for a horrible moment Kallie thought it was the footsteps of more Enchanted, but then as more people joined in, she realised it was applause. The audience and the villagers were cheering. The Wildstormers started to clap too, laughing and whooping. Kallie looked around her and, at long last, she felt her heart sing with triumph.

CHAPTER THIRTY-THREE

That night, the Wildstormers had a bonfire in the meadow. The sky glittered with stars and the Hay Moon shone like a pearl.

The cast curled around the bonfire in sleeping bags and blankets. There was a low hum of chatter and the peaceful crackling of flames. Most of the parents were staying in the local inn in Merricombe, leaving the Wildstormers to their night of celebrations. Kallie's mum was getting the train up from London the next day; she hadn't been able to get the time off work for the show.

Kallie, Emilia, Marlow and Arley sat slightly apart from everyone, leaning against Kallie's tent. Burn had brought down a barbeque and everyone was munching on homemade burgers – veggie for Kallie and Arley – with caramelised onions, spicy relish and pickles. Kallie didn't think she'd ever tasted anything so delicious.

The King's Downfall had been a tremendous success. The audience had been made up of families and friends and a few villagers, who'd come to heckle but ended up getting caught up in the story. Even the villagers who'd been protesting outside were gushing with praise, all thoughts of the witch's curse and the villagers' distrust of Wildstorm forgotten. Everyone agreed that it had been the best special effects they'd ever seen in a theatre.

'That explosion at the end!' one husband had remarked to his wife. 'The way that little boy pulled off that monster costume – quick as lightning!'

'Yes, dear. They do it all with trapdoors and loud bangs,' said his wife patronisingly.

Even the cast thought it had been a spectacular ending but a few were a little peeved that they hadn't been able to try on the demon costume.

Kallie felt light with joy. She was content to sit and listen to the others, letting their victory wash over her like the warmth of the fire. Emilia was back to her normal self – as was everyone else – irrepressibly cheerful to have Arley back, and her energy was infectious. She and Marlow were busy telling Arley what had happened over the last week. Marlow kept leaping to his feet to demonstrate how he'd thrown the sword to Kallie's aid or mime driving the golf cart at breakneck speed.

'But Kallie was the real hero,' Marlow acknowledged, sitting down to finish his burger. 'It was pretty cool when you made the Wrathlok explode.'

'Wow! Must be so tough to admit you weren't the star of the show for once!' teased Emilia.

Marlow stuck out his tongue.

'What did your mum think about your – er – alternative ending to the play?' asked Arley.

'She hasn't mentioned it,' said Emilia, biting her lip. 'Everyone else seems to have taken it in their stride – even if they are a little confused by it all.'

'No one would want to believe that a *real* demon broke into the theatre,' muttered Marlow. 'I don't even want to believe it myself.'

He gave an involuntary shudder.

'People are funny like that.' Emilia grinned. 'Put something slap-bang in their face and if they don't want to believe in it, they don't even blink.'

'You know Ivan's staying in Hollowstar House tonight,' said Marlow. 'Violet's sitting with him. Apparently, he's very confused.'

'Hope he recovers,' said Kallie, leaning forward. 'I feel terrible.'

'He'll be fine,' reassured Emilia. 'Don't feel bad. You saved him! I wonder who the demon disguised himself as in Ellsabet's time.'

'Maybe the innkeeper?' said Kallie, thinking back to Rose's letter and the page from Ellsabet's witch trial, for which the innkeeper had given evidence. 'We'll probably never know for sure.'

'Still pretty gross, though. The whole "wearing a human" thing,' said Emilia, squirming. 'Now I remember when Ivan – I mean the Wrathlok – tried to enchant me in the fencing class. Ivan sort of stumbled and grabbed my arm; next thing I knew, I woke up on the theatre floor. If it wasn't for the witch's marks, I'd have been a goner! Then in The Ferns, when you guys weren't looking, he came up behind me and held on to my wrist – before I could say anything, everything went black.'

'You felt like you were in a dream,' said Arley, 'like you weren't sure if you were awake or asleep.'

'It was a hell of a headache,' agreed Emilia, licking relish from her fingers.

'We could hear his voice giving us orders,' said Arley, nodding. 'But on Fallow Hill' – he looked at Kallie – 'I started hearing your voice too.'

'Really?' Kallie felt a little apologetic. 'I think when

he tried to enchant me, he connected me with all of the Enchanted by accident.'

'He didn't know who he was dealing with!' Emilia smirked. 'Trying to battle the great Storyteller!'

Kallie's face grew hot. She still wasn't completely comfortable with the idea of being the hero. She looked at Arley, keen to change the subject away from her.

'How did the Wrathlok get you? It must have been in the woods, right?'

'Yeah. I was actually on my way to Wildstorm.' He looked at Emilia. 'My dad didn't want me to be in the play, you know he doesn't really understand theatre stuff, but your mum said she'd keep a place open for me if I wanted it. My parents wouldn't even have had to pay for it.'

'She's all right, my mum.' Emilia grinned.

'I thought maybe I could sneak away and join rehearsals without my dad knowing. Well, anyway, I just wanted to talk to you about it first.' He looked down at his burger. 'I'm sorry I stopped messaging you. I didn't know what to say. Then, well . . .'

'Getting enchanted by a demon is a fair excuse.' Emilia smiled. 'I'm glad I've got you back now. You'll always be a Stormer.'

'Oh, just hug already!' huffed Marlow, rolling his

eyes, and everyone laughed.

Emilia pulled Arley into a one-armed hug, getting ketchup all over his jacket. She caught Kallie's eye and mouthed 'Thank you.' Kallie beamed back.

'Anyone want more food?' said Emilia, breaking away from Arley, her cheeks a little flushed.

'Go on, then.' Kallie grinned, scrambling to her feet.

The two of them skirted the bonfire; Marlow's friends Sabina and Tilly leapt up to tell Kallie, for the fourth time, how much they'd loved her speech and how they'd always said she wasn't a cheat. Kallie thanked them and hurried after Emilia to the barbeque where Burn was sizzling more burgers. There was a bucket at his feet, full to the brim with more sauces and relishes than Kallie could name.

'Well, here are the surprise stars of the show.' Kallie looked up to see Jackie standing over them, the firelight throwing shadows over her narrow face. 'I remember telling you two that you were banned from the play. Or was that just in my imagination?'

The two of them looked at each other. Kallie suddenly felt nervous; after everything they'd been through, were they about to get into *more* trouble?

'Mum, it was an emergency,' said Emilia.

Jackie raised an eyebrow, but Kallie thought she

seemed more amused than annoyed. And she had a sudden thought.

'You found Ellsabet's play in the costume chamber, didn't you?' asked Kallie. 'In that old chest.'

'Indeed I did.' Jackie nodded. 'It is my duty to know the secrets of my theatre. The chest was sealed shut so it was no easy feat. Someone had been very careful to keep it safe. Such a shame the last page has been lost to history.'

'Well, actually, we found it.' Kallie unfolded the missing script from her pocket and handed it over. 'If you want to keep it.'

Jackie's face shone with excitement; for a second Kallie thought she might cry. Jackie took the page with trembling fingers, blinking very fast, and gave Kallie a brisk nod of thanks.

'Do you know what happened to Ellsabet Graveheart's sister-in-law?' asked Kallie gently. 'I think her name was Rose. Rose Graveheart.'

'Rose Graveheart?' Jackie looked curiously between them. 'Rose Graveheart is the name of a little-known seventeenth-century poet and governess who worked in London until 1632. Her connection to Merricombe is not widely known.'

'Well, Merricombe should change its name to

Rose-Town!' Emilia burst out, unable to control herself. 'Rose is the reason we saved Wildstorm – saved everyone – only it was Kallie, she's Ellsabet's successor! The new Storyteller! She fought a real demon with her words! The curse—'

'That sounds a little far-fetched, Emilia.' Jackie tutted, but Kallie thought she saw a mischievous smile flicker across her face. 'There's no denying that the play has been a triumph,' she continued. 'It's the talk of the village and I believe I have you to thank for that. A few villagers have already asked me about putting on a play in the spring with adults playing the parts – the vicar is particularly enthusiastic. And Mr Mildew came to apologise for the Historical Society's treatment of Wildstorm over the past week. He looked very strange, rather like he'd been rolling around in the dirt.'

'So we're not being punished?' said Emilia hopefully and Jackie shook her head slowly.

'Not this time.'

Jackie must have been grateful, because she permitted Emilia and Arley to stay in the campsite that night. They all shared Marlow's bell-tent, squeezed together in their sleeping bags with blankets and extra cushions. Emilia snuck up to Hollowstar House and returned with a giant box of chocolate cookies and Smudge tucked under her arm. Smudge found a comfortable spot on Kallie's feet and went to sleep. The chattering and munching went on into the early hours of the morning. When she did at last fall asleep, Kallie slept with a smile.

The next morning dawned clear and sweet. Yawning and bleary-eyed, Kallie, Emilia, Marlow and Arley followed Smudge up the path from the campsite. It was their last breakfast at Wildstorm Theatre Camp. Although still as crotchety as ever, Burn had made a feast of buttermilk pancakes and bacon and fried halloumi cheese. Kallie still felt pretty guilty for fighting him – even if he was being controlled by an evil demon at the time.

The breakfast went by too quickly. Soon parents arrived to collect their kids and to help pack up and hunt for lost shoes. Ivan's dad arrived with chocolates and sweets, beaming with pride at his son's performance. Ivan was looking more himself and finished off four pancakes while his dad fussed around him. He waved goodbye to Kallie as he left, still looking a little confused. She hoped he wouldn't have any ill effects after the Wrathlok's possession.

Maybe it was the lack of sleep, but everything felt surreal to Kallie as she watched everyone rushing about. She felt like Wildstorm was only just beginning for her and a panicked loneliness rose inside her. Then, through the crowd, Kallie spotted her mum.

'Kallie! Babe, come here.' her mum swept her up in her arms. 'Puck and Mustard-Seed send their love; they've eaten one of your socks again but I'll buy you a new pair.'

Kallie felt a lump in her throat as she clung on to her mum, almost overwhelmed by the rush of homesickness and love.

'Violet was just telling me what a star you've been,' said her mum.

'Oh right. She didn't mention anything else, did she?' said Kallie, nervously.

'Just that it's been a pleasure having you at Wildstorm this year. Why? Did anything bad happen?' her mum quizzed.

'Oh no.' Kallie grinned. 'Of course not!'

Kallie wanted to hold back time but all too soon everyone was hugging and sharing tearful goodbyes. Many of the Wildstormers waved to Kallie and congratulated her again on the spectacular surprise ending.

'Seriously?' whispered Emilia. 'They honestly think my mum planned a massive surprise ending without rehearsing it! Haven't they met her?'

'Hopefully see you next summer,' said Arley, hugging Kallie, 'when I'm more myself.'

'Thanks for saving our lives and all that,' said Marlow, nudging Kallie with his elbow.

'I couldn't have done it without you.' Kallie smiled. 'I think we make a good team.'

'Yes, but, as Emilia said, you're the real star of the show.' Marlow smiled back. 'Catch you later, Storyteller!'

Kallie watched Marlow walk away between his parents and grinned to herself. He wasn't so bad, Marlow. She felt Emilia pluck at her sleeve and her friend gave her a mischievous look.

'Come on! You can't go without saying goodbye.'

Kallie glanced at her mum, who was laughing with Ray, the set designer; she wouldn't miss her for a while. So Kallie followed Emilia down the side of Hollowstar House, through the trees and back to the theatre. Smudge tiptoed behind them, his tail flicking importantly.

Kallie was surprised to see that the doors to the theatre looked unharmed by last night's escapades.

Emilia slipped the key into the lock and it creaked open. The chairs had been pushed to the sides and the set had been half dismantled. The backdrop had been replaced by a white canvas once more. Kallie gazed up at the witch's marks in the beams; they were barely visible in the sunlight. It felt so strange to imagine the adventure that had happened right there, only yesterday.

'So was Ellsabet really a witch?' said Emilia, jumping up to sit on the side of the stage, her legs dangling.

'I don't think she had any real magic, not like the Wrathlok,' said Kallie, joining her. 'She just used everything she'd learnt about him to work out a way to stop him.'

'But the quill literally flew in the air and covered the Wrathlok in all those words!' marvelled Emilia. 'That was actual magic, right?'

'I guess so,' said Kallie, watching Smudge walking around the edge of the theatre. 'I didn't do anything – it was all the quill and maybe the theatre helped.' The light filtering through the high windows seemed to wink at her. 'I think . . . I think Ellsabet knew that stories and plays have a kind of magic. Those dreams I had about the quill and knowing the play

266

before I read it, I suppose that was some strange bond with Ellsabet?'

'Sounds like magic to me,' said Emilia. 'But one more thing. We'll never know for certain if the story about Ellsabet in Rose's letter was . . . well . . . true. Will we?'

'I don't think it matters,' said Kallie slowly. 'Stories aren't really about telling the truth . . . I think the important thing is how a story makes you feel.'

'Spoken like a true storyteller,' said Emilia in a mock-wise voice. 'You know, I'm glad you came to Wildstorm, I know the return of a new Storyteller woke up a mind-sucking demon and all that but if you hadn't come, then . . .' Emilia suddenly went very red.

'What?'

'I would never have found my best friend,' Emilia mumbled, bright as a beetroot.

Kallie grinned, then laughed – which made Emilia laugh. The two of them snorted with laughter together.

'Emilia! Kallie!' Jackie was standing in the doorway. 'It's time to go.'

Smudge hurried to Jackie's side, purring loudly. Kallie and Emilia slipped off the stage and walked over to her. Kallie found herself counting each step, her final moments at Wildstorm that summer.

'Kallie, I have something for you,' said Jackie. 'It has lived in Hollowstar House for many hundreds of years but in light of recent events I think you should keep it.'

She was holding out the green quill, battered and broken.

'I – are you sure? Th – thank you,' stammered Kallie, taking the quill and twirling it through her fingers.

'That speech you did last night . . .' Jackie gave her a thin smile. 'I rather liked it. Perhaps, in a few years' time, the Wildstorm Theatre Camp will be performing a play by the great Kallie Tamm herself.'

Kallie blushed scarlet and looked at her shoes.

'Yes! You've got to start writing us a play.' Emilia beamed and Smudge rubbed against Kallie's ankles in agreement. 'The second you get home – no, the second you get on the train! We can rehearse it on the phone. Marlow's in and Arley too. Obviously give me the best lines!'

Kallie laughed.

'Yeah, all right.' She grinned. 'I think I've got a few ideas.'

And, with one last look back, Kallie closed the theatre doors behind them. Their footsteps faded away and inside the building all was silent. It was as if the theatre was holding its breath. The sunlight fell in dusty spirals on the empty stage, waiting peacefully for the next story that would bring it to life again.

Acknowledgements

Just like Kallie, when I was twelve years old, I was diagnosed with dyslexia. At first, I was distraught because I thought it meant I couldn't become an author, but dyslexia hasn't stopped me writing stories and getting published. When I was younger, I spent a lot of my time writing plays and (like Emilia) I loved acting. I loved how you could step into a story and, for a few hours, make-believe that it was real.

Every summer, between the ages of fifteen and seventeen, I took part in a theatre summer camp in Gloucestershire called Barnstorm (you may find the name familiar). Had it not been for those magnificent productions and joyful memories, I would never have written this book. So thank you to everyone involved in Barnstorm – Tessa, Jo B, the whole crew – and thank you to Shona, Jamie, Sam and Leo for inviting this Londoner to join the fun.

There are many people who helped *The Wildstorm Curse* become the book it is today – the show could not have gone on without each and every one of them.

Thank you to my agent, Louise Lamont – thank you for your extraordinary wisdom and humour and your infectious enthusiasm.

Thank you to my editor, Jenna Mackintosh, and editorial team Ruth Girmatsion, Becca Allen and Adele Brimacombe who have done a spectacular job directing my story and making it shine. Michelle Brackenborough, thank you for your vision for the cover and incredible designed elements within the book; Paola Escobar, thank you for bringing my characters alive with your cover artwork. And thank you Kristyna Litten for drawing the gorgeous map of Merricombe. Thank you Emily Thomas, publicist unparalleled in energy and brilliance; thank you Fiona Evans and Kristina Hill for your creative marketing; Hannah Bradridge for that pizza-book-signing session. And thank you to everyone at Hachette Children's who have helped this book along the way – from Sales to Rights to Production – I applaud you all!

Thank you to author friends who have inspired and supported me with my writing – including Jamie Littler, Katherine Woodfine, Abi Elphinstone, Michelle Harrison, Liz Kessler, A.F. Steadman, Jack Meggitt-Phillips, Katie Tsang, Danny Wallace – your kind words have helped more than I can say.

Thank you to the friends who sparked my love of theatre and make-believe; Sorcha and Rò. Thank you to the Friend Folk who helped me get started on this new story.

To my best (and only) sister, Alice, I put the jokes in for you, thanks for always being my favourite audience member. Pirate the cat for sitting on my lap and being the inspiration for Smudge. Mum and Dad, thank you for always believing in me and backing every crazy creative idea I've ever had!

Finally thank you to everyone who has supported my books – to all the librarians, teachers, booksellers and readers – you have shown me that storytelling is powerful. It doesn't matter if you're bad at spelling or stumble when you read, all that matters is the story you choose to share.

'AT FIRST LAYAH THOUGHT IT WAS BIRDSONG – A HIGH THIN SOUND, RISING AND FALLING. AND EACH NIGHT, IT RETURNED.'

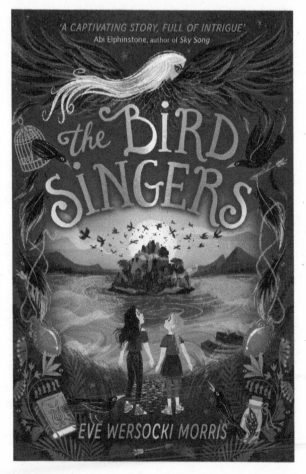

'A CAPTIVATING STORY, FULL OF INTRIGUE'
Abi Elphinstone, author of Sky Song

the BIRD SINGERS

EVE WERSOCKI MORRIS

Strange things are happening to Layah and her sister. A peculiar whistling in their lonely cottage, a handful of unusual feathers, murmurings of a shadow in the forest. And Mum is acting oddly.

Layah's head is full of old myths and fairy tales from her Polish grandma, Babcia. As she starts to uncover dark secrets, she realises there's a chance these myths might be real. Time is running out to solve the mystery . . . how far will Layah go to save her family?

AUTHOR PHOTOGRAPH © YELLOWBELLY

EVE WERSOCKI MORRIS

Eve grew up in North London and has been making up stories her whole life. Despite being diagnosed with dyslexia aged twelve, she has not let that stop her literary ambitions and wrote her first full novel aged thirteen. Her debut children's book *The Bird Singers* was a *Sunday Times* Children's Book of the Week.

She spent her childhood writing plays and acting in them with her friends. For several years, she attended Barnstorm Youth Theatre Camp in Gloucestershire. It was fond memories of energetic rehearsals, 'biscuits and squash' in the garden and frantic line-learning which first inspired *The Wildstorm Curse*.

@MzEvieMo @eve_wersocki
evewersockimorris.co.uk